P9-DEG-831

HARLEQUIN®
Presents

Welcome to the new collection of Harlequin
Presents!

Don't miss contributions from favorite authors
Michelle Reid, Kim Lawrence and Susan Napier,
as well as the second part of Jane Porter's
THE DESERT KINGS series, Lucy Gordon's
passionate Italian, Chantelle Shaw's Tuscan
tycoon and Jennie Lucas's sexy Spaniard! And
look out for Trish Wylie's brilliant debut
Presents book, *Her Bedroom Surrender!*

We'd love to hear what you think about Harlequin
Presents. E-mail us at Presents@hmb.co.uk or join
in the discussions at www.iheartpresents.com
and www.sensationalromance.blogspot.com,
where you'll also find more information about
books and authors!

Susan Napier
ACCIDENTAL MISTRESS

TAKEN BY THE
MILLIONAIRE

HARLEQUIN®

TORONTO • NEW YORK • LONDON
AMSTERDAM • PARIS • SYDNEY • HAMBURG
STOCKHOLM • ATHENS • TOKYO • MILAN • MADRID
PRAGUE • WARSAW • BUDAPEST • AUCKLAND

ISBN-13: 978-0-373-12729-0
ISBN-10:   0-373-12729-4

ACCIDENTAL MISTRESS

First North American Publication 2008.

www.eHarlequin.com

Printed in U.S.A.

All about the author...
Susan Napier

SUSAN NAPIER is a former journalist and
scriptwriter who turned to writing romance fiction
after her two sons were born. She lives in Auckland,
New Zealand, with her journalist husband, who
generously provides the ongoing inspiration for her
fictional heroes, and two temperamental cats, whose
curious paws contribute the occasional typographical
error when they join her at the keyboard. Born on
St. Valentine's Day, Susan feels that it was her destiny
to write romances, and, having written over thirty-five
books for Harlequin, she still loves the challenges of
working within the genre. She likes writing traditional
tales with a twist, and believes that to keep romance
alive you have to keep the faith—to believe in love.
Not just in the romantic kind of love that pervades
her books, but in the everyday, caring-and-sharing
kind of love that builds enduring relationships. Susan's
extended family is scattered over the globe, which is
fortunate, as she enjoys traveling and seeking out new
experiences to fuel her flights of imagination.

Susan loves to hear from readers and can be
contacted by e-mail through the Web site at
www.harlequinpresents.com.

Look out for Susan Napier's next book,
Public Scandal, Private Mistress
in November, only from Harlequin Presents!

CHAPTER ONE

BY THE TIME Emily Quest realised what sort of party it was, it was too late to storm out in a fit of moral outrage.

After all, she had lied and cheated her way into this exclusive den of iniquity for her own less-than-honest purposes, so it would be hypocritical to condemn her fellow guests for *their* immoral behaviour.

And, dressed as she was in the height of trash-fashion, it was hard to blame anyone but herself for the obnoxious kind of attention she was having to endure. Playing the brainless bimbo had been an essential part of her hastily conceived plan, but unfortunately it had pitched her headlong into situations she was ill-equipped to handle.

At least she was wearing underwear, she consoled herself, which was more than she could say about some of the other girls who had been invited along to liven up the party for the unattached males! A number of them were from a well-known local escort service but others were merely "gifted amateurs", as Emily's hairdresser—from whom she had conned her invitation—had cheerfully put it. Chasing trophy males on the private-party circuit was apparently a hotly-contested competitive sport in some social circles.

Emily collected her drinks from the self-serve bar, averting her gaze from the crystal bowl of pills being touted with brazen effrontery by a baby-faced young man with a fake American accent and a large diamond stud winking in his ear. Given the nature of her invitation she had been braced for a certain degree of sophisticated decadence, but she was shocked at the squalor of some of the goings-on. If this was the way the rich and not-so-famous carried on behind closed doors, no wonder society was in trouble!

She doubted that the absent owners of the luxurious water-front mansion in the middle of Auckland's "Millionaires' Row" had given their house-sitting adult son permission to run drug-riddled orgies while they cruised the Mediterranean but, given what she knew of their snobbery, she had a depressing feeling that they would be more disgusted by the questionable social status of many of the guests than the rampant abuse of drugs and alcohol and sexual promiscuity. Junior and his friends obviously liked to spice up their lives of gross overprivilege by walking on the wild side, if the number of patched gang members hanging around in raucous thickets of denim and leather were anything to go by. More unsettling still, some of the tattooed hulks were employed as de facto security guards and bouncers, and the casual vandalism that was being carried out in the name of having a good time gave Emily a renewed sense of urgency about her mission. She just needed to hold onto her nerve for a little while longer…

Pinning on a brilliant smile to mask her growing unease, Emily wove her way through the overcrowded pool room which was serving as a bar, holding the two brimming glasses and square bottle above her head as she squeezed between well-fuelled party-goers screaming at each other over the driving dance music that pulsated through the walls.

Her hopes of a quick exit had long since faded and her head was starting to ache with the noise and the tension of pretend-ing to enjoy herself, the spiky brown curls that normally formed a jaunty halo above her heart-shaped face wilting in the claus-trophobic heat. A haze of smoke had made her tear-ducts sting and robbed her sky-blue eyes of their eager sparkle. The only thing she was eager to do right now was get back to her semi-incoherent host, do what she had to do, and leave.

Unfortunately, the intoxicated state that made him so suggestible was off-set by an infuriating inability to concentrate. After offering her a tour around the opulent splendour of the private wing locked away from the rest of the party, he kept getting sidetracked by his baser impulses—and just when Emily had finally laid eyes on her goal she had been sent off to act as barmaid!

The monotonous throb of the music poured out through the network of ceiling-mounted speakers, pursuing her with relentless insistence as she pressed her way back through the heaving mob of people jamming the marble hallway. Even the polished floor beneath her slender high heels seemed to vibrate, and it didn't help her progress to discover that the polished surface was already dangerously slick with spilled drinks and a scattering of broken glass.

Emily skirted the door to the ground-floor bathroom where she had earlier blundered in on two glamorous, model-thin waifs bent over streaks of white powder on the onyx vanity. Their giggling invitation to join them had been punctuated by the hoarse cries of an anonymous man and his stridently vocal sex partner making boisterous use of the adjoining toilet cubical. Mentally scrubbing away at the sordid memory, Emily concentrated on pushing past the jiggling throng at the entrance to the formal lounge where a DJ was pumping up the volume. A stray elbow jabbed her in the kidney and she stumbled, shunting up against a sweaty, over-excited male who took the accidental thrust of her breasts as an open invitation to paw at her plunging cleavage.

Her laden hands trapped aloft by the crush, Emily was momentarily helpless against his clumsy lechery. She jerked her head aside from the wet-lipped lunge of the stranger's mouth, uttering a furious cry of protest as she squirmed away from a bruising hand groping up under the short skirt of her black lace dress. No one seemed to notice or care what was happening to her and for an awful moment she thought she was going to be violated right there amongst the bobbing dancers.

Fear and anger kicked her self-protective instincts into action and she threw up a driving knee, gratified to feel it strike home with crushing force. Her violent recoil tilted her wrists and squeals and curses erupted when a cascade of ice-cubes jounced out of the glasses to hail down on the surrounding heads, including that of her erstwhile assailant.

'Sorry!' Emily yelled insincerely, relieved to feel herself yanked backwards out of the dangerous mêlée by a big hand hooking into the belt of her wraparound dress and swinging her around the corner into a relatively less-crowded arm of the branching hall.

She lowered her aching arms and smiled gratefully up at her saviour, clutching the dripping glasses and slippery bottle close to her over-exposed chest, well away from his superbly cut black suit and crisp white shirt front. At five feet six Emily didn't consider herself to be short, but even in high heels she had to crank her neck back to see higher than the sharp jut of his smooth-shaven jaw above the immaculate collar. Unfortunately, the fresh spatters of moisture on her thickly applied mascara were causing it to clump, making it increasingly difficult to pry her eyelashes apart and interfering with her vision.

'Thanks—' she said breathlessly, still shaken by her struggle, rapidly blinking to try to untangle her sticky black lashes and focus properly on his face.

She succeeded just in time to see him turn his back and walk away, and with a shock she registered the look of cold contempt on his hard features. It was like a sharp slap in the face, cutting off the nervous laugh that had bubbled to her lips and leaving her stranded in embarrassment.

For a few moments after he disappeared she stood rooted to the spot, trying to convince herself that she had misread her fleeting glimpse of his expression, but the vivid impression of a pair of steel-blue eyes iced with disdain remained graphically clear in her memory.

Her cheeks burned as if the slap had been physical. He hadn't even lingered long enough to acknowledge her thanks. Perhaps he had been regretting coming to her rescue—or having second thoughts about whether she had required rescuing at all! Perhaps he had judged her a sexual tease who had bitten off more than she could chew...the type of woman who got off on flaunting herself at a man until he lost control. He had probably thought that her wildly batting eyes and breathless voice had been her crass attempt at a sexy come-on.

But this isn't really me! she wanted to rush after him and explain.

Then she berated herself for caring. What did it matter what anyone at this wretched party thought of her current guise? It wasn't as if she was likely to run into any of them again, and even if she did they wouldn't recognise her as her normal, everyday self.

Emily gripped the slippery drinks with renewed determination and doggedly pushed on towards the rear of the house. Okay, so perhaps she had overcompensated a trifle with the blatantly sexual combination of black fishnet tights, shiny stilettos and ultra-short, take-me-off dress, but she had known that she couldn't rely on her rather ordinary face and old-fashioned good manners to get her where she had needed to be tonight. She had already tried the ladylike approach and been rebuffed. She couldn't wait any longer.

Tonight was literally her last chance to repay the enormous debt of gratitude she owed her grandfather. If she succeeded, it would have been well worth the temporary humiliation, and if not—well, at least she would know she had tried her best...

With that thought in mind she found the courage to face down the huge, muscle-bound Neanderthal who tried to stop her entering the short hall that led to the family wing.

'Party's back that way,' he growled, planting a grimy black boot on the wall in front of her, barring her way with his beefy leg, and pointing his bottle of beer over her shoulder.

She wisely forbore to point out that he was scuffing the paint-work. 'I'm with the *private* party,' she reminded him with a re-proachful pout. 'I went out for more drinks?' Her plaintive upward lilt encouraged his tiny brain to make the connection.

'Oh, yeah, that was you,' he grunted, lowering his leg with a heavy thud. 'So what took you so long?'

She imagined pouring the bottle over his dreadlocked head and gave him a dazzling smile. 'There was big a queue for the toilet.'

'Huh?' His eyebrows crawled like hairy caterpillars across his jutting forehead. 'Oh—I get it,' he said, his beady eyes lightening with an evil grin. 'Did you bring enough for me?'

Oh, God, he thought she was talking about drugs! she realised, her smile dimming. 'Sorry—maybe next trip,' she blurted recklessly, sashaying towards the solid, wood-sheathed metal door at the far end of the hall.

'Have fun! I know Mikey is big into girl-on-girl when he's hammered!' His meaty chuckle made her skin shrink as she levered open the door-handle with her elbow and slipped inside.

There were no speakers installed here, and the sounds of the party barely penetrated the thick walls and heavy door of the opulently furnished 'safe' room.

Her eyes flew immediately to the polished side table against the wall opposite the white leather couch. The blue and white porcelain 'pilgrim' flask was still there, small and unobtrusive, its delicate beauty quite beneath the notice of the other four occupants of the lamp-lit room.

Thank goodness it hadn't been placed in one of the glass-fronted cabinets that lined the room, she thought as she crossed to the man lolling on the couch.

Emily knew he was thirty but Michael Webber—'Mikey' to his less salubrious friends—looked at least a decade younger, his thin face almost formless in its lack of character. He accepted the drink she handed him with a foolish grin and an unsteady hand.

'Sorry you had to wait but it's a madhouse out there,' she murmured.

'No worries, babe…' he drawled, snagging the bottle as well, and Emily saw that there were indeed none as far as he was concerned; beneath his floppy fringe his eyes were at half-mast, revealing the tell-tale pinpoint narrowness of his pupils. He had merely been on a drunken high when she'd left, but now he was skimming the edge of the stratosphere. Emily glanced at the chief suspect, the shrink-wrapped, bleached blonde sitting on his lap, who glared her defiance and beckoned for the remaining glass with long red talons.

'I'll take that,' she said, gloating over Emily's demotion to mere waitress.

Mickey made a slightly incoherent toast to the girl in his lap, and the redhead and brunette snuggled up on either side of him— the little entourage he had collected along his meandering tour, and whom he had been cruelly playing off against each other all evening. Typically, he appeared not to remember any of their names, but addressed them all as 'babe'. Emily's opinion of him sank even lower as he topped up all their glasses and urged: 'Bottoms up, girls—literally I hope!'

They all giggled madly at that, except Emily, who realised that the drug-taking session in her absence had rendered her the outsider of the group. At the moment they were all ignoring her, giving her the message that she was superfluous to their fun and games, but she didn't know how long she could trust that to last. At least she could be confident that none of them was in any condition to be reliable witnesses if anything went wrong.

Conscious that she still had to stay in character, Emily put on a sulky expression and flounced over to the handbag she had left tucked safely out of sight behind a boxy white armchair. She made a big production of her annoyance as she carefully delved, muttering, into the stygian depths of the stiff-sided, black leather bag. By the time she had produced a cheap lipstick and mirrored compact, Mickey had embarked on one of his long, rambling, pointless stories and the three women were twining around him like snakes. Emily moved closer to the table with the flask, ostensibly to take advantage of the better lighting focused on the monochromatic modern canvas on the wall.

Blocking the view from the couch with her back, she lowered her open handbag to the level of the polished surface. Her heart skipping, she reached in and removed the lid of the rigid brown box wedged into the centre of her bag with a thick padding of bubble wrap. Her nerves were jumping but she was proud to see that her hand was as steady as a rock. Used to handling very fine and fragile objects, her slender fingers skilfully peeled back the layers of acid-free tissue paper and lifted the small blue and white flask out of its soft nest of expanded polystyrene.

With a smooth action she had practised over and over in her studio at home, she placed the arched flask onto the table top with delicate precision and almost simultaneously scooped up the one that had been standing there. It was small enough to fit in the palm of her hand, but conscious of the stickiness on her skin she held it only with the tips of her fingers. With a frisson, her sharp, professional eye found and traced the barely detectable line that indicated a poorly repaired break. It was already starting to discolour and in time would become obvious even to the un-initiated. Anger momentarily blotted out her sense of self-pres-ervation as she stared down at the evidence of her betrayal.

Jolted back to awareness by a brief hush behind her, she quickly lowered the flask into the lined box in her bag, glancing sideways to encounter a familiar pair of coldly condemning blue eyes watching her from the open doorway, directly in line with her position.

Dismay froze her face while her fingers continued to work blindly, refolding the protective layer of tissue over the porce-lain and guiding the lid back onto the box. She saw the elegant stranger's grim gaze shift from the flask on the table to her hand as it withdrew from the depths of her bag, innocently clutching the plastic compact and shiny lipstick case.

How long had he been standing there, and how much had he actually seen? Had those arctic eyes watched the whole, sly exchange, or had he just arrived to catch the tail-end of her furtive movements?

Unfortunately he looked as sober as a judge and twice as cen-sorious, but then, as Emily well knew—appearances could be deceptive. She put him at about thirty, nearly a decade older than herself, but his pale, angular features were stamped with more than an extra decade's worth of arrogance.

Was he really as stern and stuffy as his flinty face and austere formality would suggest? If so, what was he doing at a party like this in the first place?

The panicked questions tumbled through Emily's mind as she forced herself to click the incriminating bag closed, open her compact and start applying the garish, blood-red lipstick with feigned self-absorption.

Bracing herself for his ringing denunciation, she held her breath as he stepped into the room, and glanced over to see the grinning Neanderthal in the hall behind him, tucking a red banknote into his jeans pocket as he backed away from the self-closing door.

A hundred-dollar bribe?

Oh, God, thought Emily, *this cannot be good!*

She hurriedly finished glossing her mouth, rolling her lips together to disguise the slightly ragged outline where her hand had begun a betraying tremble.

Nerves shredding, she checked the intruder out through her heavy lashes as she dropped the make-up into the side-pocket of her bag and settled the strap securely over her shoulder. Sure enough, her humming instincts were right—he was still watching her with a chiselled frown, suspicion and disapproval oozing from every arrogant pore. But at least he wasn't pointing an accusing finger.

Perhaps he *hadn't* seen anything after all. Perhaps he didn't realise she was as guilty as sin, and his reaction was purely a hangover from their previous encounter. He had dismissed her as beneath his notice then...perhaps he could be goaded into doing it again.

Recklessly she lifted her head and took the offensive, staring openly back at him and forming her ultra-shiny red mouth into a slow, extravagant mockery of an air-kiss.

Then, swinging her hips, she sashayed over to him and flipped a derisive finger at his fastidious black tie.

'A little overdressed for our private orgy, aren't you?' she taunted huskily.

He caught her finger in a controlled grip, and slowly forced it back down to her side. A wicked thrill ripped through her body at his commmanding touch and she felt him stiffen, a tiny blue flame flickering in the iceberg eyes.

She leaned closer, until the tips of her breasts brushed his jacket, and added the final insult: 'Or did you just pay to watch?'

Later she would shudder at the foolish risk she had taken, but her bold tactics worked. The ice-floes moved back in and smothered the spark of fire.

'I don't consider sex a spectator sport,' he said bluntly, in a voice like sharpened flint. 'Nor is it something I pay for. So, if you'll excuse me, I have a few questions for your gracious host, and then I'll leave you to it.'

And with that sarcastic little jab he walked around her to start a low-pitched conversation with a befuddled and increasingly defensive-looking Mikey.

Emily was free!

Free to walk out of the room, out of the house, and out of a world of trouble.

CHAPTER TWO

EMILY nudged her borrowed car around the rising bend and floored the accelerator, leaning forwards as if her shifting body weight could help push the aging engine up the final hill. Perhaps this was one of those rare times when a few extra pounds could prove to be an advantage!

The engine's high-pitched whine became a labouring scream as she ground painfully towards the brow. She gripped the steering wheel and prayed she wasn't about to blow something vital and start hurtling backwards down the narrow, winding road. Apart from the fact that the car was only on loan, her credit with insurance companies was rock-bottom right now. She didn't need another accident to add to her current set of worries.

She sighed with relief when she saw the distinctive stone pillars topped with unique, hand-blown glass light-globes rise into view, turning thankfully into the paved driveway edged with flowering trees and shrubs and letting the car coast gently down towards the large turning circle at the front portico.

Built of white stone, the long, low Nash house was perched on the high point of a ridge that had once been open farmland. Over the last half-century the lush pastures and stands of native bush on the northern side had been gradually nibbled away by the creeping urban sprawl of New Zealand's largest city, while along the ridge and its hilly surrounds the council by-laws had limited subdivision to five-acre "lifestyle" blocks that eased the transition from town to country.

The house itself was sited on the footprint of the original farmhouse, commanding views south across rolling green farmland and market gardens as far as the distant smudge of the Bombay Hills, thirty kilometres away, and north over the marching tracts of suburbia to the commercial centre of Auckland where skyscrapers were stacked like toy blocks to the edge of the blue-green waters of the Waitemata Harbour.

Peter Nash had built his house as a home rather than a showcase for his wealth, well before the area had become fashionable. There were plenty of other, far more palatial residences springing up along Ridge Road, where wealthy 'lifestyle block' owners could play at being countryfolk within thirty minutes' drive of the CBD, but none, Emily thought as she drove around to the side of the house, with such perfect placement and unpretentious charm.

A large part of that charm was due to the efforts of Peter's late wife, Rose, who had been an avid gardener and homemaker. She had also been a passionate collector of antique china and regularly sent pieces to Quest Restorations for cleaning and repair.

Emily parked beside the Dutch-barn-shaped garage and allowed the car to cough and shudder into respectable silence before she got out to heft a bulky carton from the crammed back seat.

The air was warm and still, laden with the sweet scents of early summer, and she took a deep, appreciative breath. It was bliss to her lungs after all the smoke-and-chemical tainted air she had inhaled earlier that morning. She paused to enjoy the single slice of panoramic view that was visible between the barn and the corner of the house. It directed her gaze down towards the beaches of the inner suburbs, and she couldn't help her eyes measuring the distance between a cluster of moored yachts and a particular crooked finger of land.

Of course, she couldn't distinguish the actual house from so far away, but somewhere in amongst that patchwork blur of buildings was the slate roof of the Webber residence. It had been two years since the hideous debacle of the Chinese flask but she still remembered every second of that infamous party as if it were yesterday. She had had nightmares for weeks before and after her desperate venture, and even now sometimes woke in a cold sweat of fear, her heart racing from the pursuit of some nameless dread. The threat of exposure had faded with the passage of time but she could never quite rid herself of the guilty notion that she had cheated fate, and she still got a queasy feeling in her stomach whenever she drove in the area. If she had learned one good thing about herself that night, it was that she was not cut out to be a criminal!

Nudging the car door closed with her hip, she carried her burden around to the front door and manoeuvred her elbow to push the doorbell, wincing a little as she identified another undiscovered bruise. While she waited she heeled off her sooty shoes and checked the soles of her white cotton socks.

'Hello, Mrs Cooper.' She smiled at the dour-faced woman who opened the door. 'I hope you don't think I should have gone around to the tradesman's entrance with this lot!'

She was slightly surprised when Kay Cooper's peppercorn-black eyes remained chary as she stood back to let her in.

'He's been waiting for you all morning, Miss Quest,' she said, pursing her thin lips, her tone just short of outright criticism.

Knowing how fiercely protective the housekeeper was of her long-time employer, Emily accepted the rebuff. Mrs Cooper had worked for the Nashes as their "daily" for more than half of her sixty years, and had earned the right to be proprietorial.

'I'm sorry, I know I'm running a bit late but I finally got permission to go back into my studio and see if there was anything I could salvage,' she explained, putting the box down on the immaculately clean tiles just inside the door. 'I'm afraid it took longer than I thought. I was going to call ahead from the car to let Mr Nash know I was on my way…but then I remembered that my mobile died in the fire,' she added with a rueful lift of her shoulders.

The shameless play for sympathy succeeded. Mrs Cooper's tight lips eased a fraction at the reminder of Emily's catastrophic loss. Her helmet of improbably black hair hardly moved as she inclined her head towards the back of the house.

'He's in his office.'

It was still called an office, in spite of the fact that little business was now conducted within its walls. Peter Nash had sold out his booming chain of hardware stores ten years before, during his wife's first, successful battle against cancer. That he had had eight more years of companionship with his beloved Rose before the cancer returned in a more aggressive form had vindicated his decision to retire when he had, but since her death he had struggled to find a purpose for himself and fill the empty gap in his life.

'Thanks. Is it all right if I leave this stuff here for now?' she asked meekly, indicating the box. If she was going to be working here for the next few weeks it wouldn't do to get offside with Mrs Cooper. Emily had always got on well with her before, so was a little puzzled at her stiff reception.

Mrs Cooper looked down her beaky nose at the carton. 'I suppose the rest of your things are in the car?'

Was there something faintly accusing in that remark? Emily's puzzlement increased. 'Well, some of them, yes…but I'll leave them there until I know where I'm going to put everything. When Mr Nash made his offer, he was rather vague about the details…'

Which, come to think of it, wasn't like him at all. At seventy-five he might no longer have the physical stamina with which he had built his business empire, but he had lost none of his mental acuity.

Mrs Cooper sniffed. 'Well, you'd better go and find out, then. He's been up and down like a jack-in-a-box looking for you to show up. It can't be doing that heart of his any good to be getting into such a state…' And with that guilt-provoking observation she turned back towards the kitchen from whence she'd come, but entrenched work habits proved too strong to ignore and she paused to add: 'I suppose you could do with a cup of tea?'

Good manners suggested Emily politely tell her not to bother, but she had the feeling that, in her current mood, the doughty old housekeeper would take the refusal of her grudging offer as a personal insult.

'Thanks, that would be lovely,' she said, summoning a cheerful smile that brightened her faintly up-tilted eyes and infused her honey-coloured skin with delicate warmth. 'I had breakfast on the run this morning and didn't have time for a drink. My mouth feels as dry as dust—I think I must have swallowed a ton of ash when I was sifting through things at the house.'

'You do look a bit as though you've been dragged through a hedge backwards,' she was duly informed.

Ah, was that the cause of her somewhat grumpy reception? Emily wondered, conscious that she probably looked more like a scruffy teenager than the mature twenty-six-year-old she was, in her baggy tee shirt and skin-tight jeans. Usually she dressed with care whenever she came to visit, choosing ladylike blouses and skirts out of respect for Peter's age and own dapper dress sense, and to try to present the image of a confident professional. But since she was here to work rather than to socialise she had needed something practical and hardwearing, although with much of her wardrobe having literally gone up in smoke her choices had been sorely limited. Her jeans, for instance, had been bought back in the days when her hips were somewhat less generous…

'Emily—there you are!'

Peter Nash was hurrying down the hall towards them, his slight limp barely detectable in his eager stride, his alert brown eyes and thick shock of white hair a vibrant contrast to his wisp-thin body. 'Was that you arriving just now in that dreadful old banger?'

His gaze flickered over her but he looked amused rather than offended. Unlike Mrs Cooper, he had visited Emily in her studio and knew that the job of restoring beauty was frequently messy. He would expect her to dress sensibly for an ordinary workday. In contrast his pale trousers were neatly creased and his discreet bow tie colour-coordinated with his shirt and navy blazer.

'Yes, it was,' she confessed with an apologetic grin. 'It belongs to the friend who's putting me up. The fire investigator rang to say he'd let me get some things out of the house this morning and Julie lent me her car to collect them. She needs it back by this afternoon, though, so it won't be lowering the tone of your neighbourhood for long!'

Peter chuckled. He claimed to be as tough as old boots, but he had a kind heart, as Emily had discovered after the death of her grandfather at the beginning of the year and her desperate struggle to make a success of her inheritance.

James Quest had had a solid-gold reputation as a skilled restorer of museum-quality ceramics but the fact that Emily had trained and worked side by side with him since she was little more than a child, and had built up her own impressive portfolio of achievements, had not been enough to convince some of their important clients that she was a talented craftswoman in her own right, perfectly competent to handle their future commissions.

'I did offer to have Jeff pick you up and drive you wherever you wanted to go,' he pointed out.

'I know, but I didn't think it would make the right impression on the insurance assessor if I swanned up in a chauffeur-driven Rolls Royce, she said wryly. 'Not when I've put in a hardship claim!'

'It wouldn't hurt him to know you have some influential friends,' said Peter, a martial glint in his eye.

'I'm sure it won't come to that,' said Emily hastily, aware of Mrs Cooper's bridling attention, and not wanting to be held responsible for setting him off on one of his crusades. 'It's early days, yet...'

But not too early for her to secretly worry about how she was going to manage if the insurance company ultimately decided against making a full payout. She had felt sick this morning when the assessor had told her it could take weeks to process her claim, given the complications that had arisen over the way the policy renewal had been handled.

It was hard to believe that it was only four nights ago that she had woken to the insistent screech of the smoke alarm in the downstairs studio, and stumbled out of bed to find a thick haze of choking smoke creeping up the stairs. Her chest tightened at the smothering memory. The house her grandparents had lived in all their married life—and the only real home that Emily had ever known—had been a rambling old place built of native hardwood timber. The lower floor and adjoining garage had been billowing flame by the time the fire-engines arrived but their quick work had managed to save the scorched upper storey at the cost of extensive fire and water damage. It remained to be seen whether the house could be repaired, or whether the structural damage had been so great that it would have to be demolished.

'What did he have to report about the cause of the fire?'

Emily sighed and ran slender fingers through her disordered brown curls, sifting a fine mist of powdered ash onto the shoulders of her teal-blue tee shirt. 'Only that it started in the studio, but they're waiting on tests to find out whether it was chemical or whether something else set the chemicals off. Part of the trouble is that the fire service is still rushed off its feet in the aftermath of Guy Fawkes night—apparently November is a big month for unexplained fires.'

'So they're thinking it could have been deliberate?' said Peter, his tufted brows beetling, his weathered face sharp with concern.

'I don't know…the assessor was asking me all kinds of questions about the way I stored my adhesives and solvents, and disposed of cleaning materials—how tidy I kept things. Grandpa James was always very careful about that sort of thing. He insisted on my putting things away properly and cleaning up every night. I would never have been so careless as to leave potentially dangerous combinations of chemicals or flammable spills lying about!' she emphasised fiercely.

'Of course not—so you needn't worry they're going to find anything to blame you with on that score,' said Peter bracingly.

'As long as they don't start my customers thinking I work on their precious treasures in an unsafe environment.' Emily sighed.

'I can't afford for the business to start haemorrhaging clients again. I'd just started to break even for the first time since Grandpa died—'

'All the more reason for you to be able to show them you've been able to continue to work. Come and see if you approve of what I've done!' He put an age-spotted hand under Emily's elbow and urged her back the way he had come, casting his housekeeper a conspiratorial look. 'Isn't it about time for a cup of tea, Coop? And how about some of your fabulous date scones—'

Her prune face puffed out a little at his outrageous flattery. 'I was just about to put the kettle on for Miss Quest. But it'll have to be low-fat muffins. You know what the doctor said.'

'Blueberry?' he asked hopefully.

She nodded. 'With bran.'

He pulled a face. 'It's come to a pretty pass when a man has to put up with grass in his feed.'

'Better eating it than pushing it up!' his housekeeper shot back as she headed for her kitchen.

Ten minutes later Emily was still stammering in shock as she wandered around the room at the back of the Dutch barn, trailing her hand over the pristine workbenches and fitted shelving. Perfect light poured in from the big, north-facing windows illuminating her stunned features as she took in the textbook layout. A double sink was installed under a row of cupboards and a dedicated air extractor sat above a small, square, perspex spray booth fixed to one of the benches. Next to a long, foam-padded table sat a wheeled trolley with a variety of tools and materials laid out on the wooden surface—craft knives and scalpels of different sizes, files and needles, artists' brushes, spatulas, tweezers and boxes of tape, cotton wool, white ceramic tiles, abrasives, tissues, fixatives, powders and plasters.

It didn't have quite everything that a restorer might use, but it was more than just a basic kit. There was even a packet of disposable gloves and a pair of safety glasses.

'W-when you said you'd give me somewhere to work until the

insurance paid out, I thought you just meant a spare room, I never expected a fully equipped studio,' she stuttered faintly, opening one of the full-length metal cabinets to see shelves of unopened containers of detergents, distilled spirits, and fixatives.

'You should know by now that I never do things by halves,' said Peter, hugely pleased by her reaction. 'That's fireproof, by the way. And I have smoke and heat detectors.' He pointed at the ceiling. 'And air-conditioning, too, so you don't have to open a window and risk anything blowing in.'

Everything looked and smelt brand-new. 'There was only a tiny window there before!' she realised. 'How on earth could you get all this done in under a week?' she squeaked, thinking of the snail-like pace of the insurance company.

'I was in the hardware trade for over thirty years,' he told her smugly. 'With the will and the right contacts anything is doable. And there are plenty of tradesmen who'll squeeze in a rush job if they get cash in the pocket rather than having to wait on an account.' He was self-made man with no formal qualifications, it was just such a can-do attitude that had seen Peter Nash build a one-man business into a multinational franchise.

Emily shook her whirling head, overwhelmed by his generosity, secretly dismayed at what she feared was an extravagant whim. 'I just can't believe you built this all just for me. This is way too much, Peter. I can never pay you back—'

'Who's asking for repayment?' he scoffed. 'This isn't just for your sake—I get to benefit, too, remember. You're going to be cleaning up all those pieces that Rose never got around to having done when she was alive. And that Chinese jar—you said that would take at least a month from start to finish. I couldn't have you doing all that work in some poky little corner without the proper tools—the Health and Safety people would have been down on me like a ton of bricks! And Rose would turn over in her grave. She always liked you, you know…thought that you would turn out to be an even better craftsman than your grandfather—said you had a real feel for the work, and the right delicate "touch".'

Emily swallowed a hard lump in her throat. As often happened when he mentioned his wife, his expression lengthened and grew wistful and she felt the strong empathetic tug that had fostered the firm friendship that had sprung up between herself and Peter over the past couple of years.

After Rose's death, Emily's grandfather had gloomily predicted that Peter would sell her valuable collection of Chinese and European hard-paste porcelain or donate it to a museum, as he had had little personal interest in ceramics. But Emily had believed that he hadn't bankrolled his wife's expensive hobby out of disinterest but out of love, and that he would not want to put something that had meant so much to her out of his life. So it had proved, and after emerging from the depths of his mourning Peter had continued to send commissions to Quest Restorations according to a preservation plan that Rose had recorded in her collection diary.

'I still think you've spent too much,' she said uneasily.

'I've got the money, haven't I? Why shouldn't I spend it on whatever I want? I can't take it with me. And it's not as if I have anyone else to spend it on…'

Emily knew it had been a source of continuing pain and disappointment for the couple that Rose had been unable to have children. 'There's your nephews—' she began.

'Huh! The elder doesn't need it, and the younger would just blow it on high living and wild schemes! They'll be getting enough of my money when I die—they don't care what I do in the meantime.'

Emily had never met the West brothers, who were the sons of Rose's dare-devil younger brother, but she had often heard him talk with pride or exasperation about their fast-paced lives, and knew from Mrs Cooper that one or other of them regularly phoned or visited, most often thirty-two-year-old Ethan, a high-end property developer, whose bedroom was always kept aired in anticipation of his unexpected comings and goings. His younger brother Dylan was more likely to show up when he was in between occupations, or to show off a flashy new acquisition. He apparently had lofty dreams but a short attention span—'ambitious in spurts' was how Peter drily described him.

'Of course they care,' she protested. 'You're their only living relative.'

He shot her an oddly intent look. 'Only by marriage, not by blood,' he muttered, surprising her with the caveat. He had never before suggested that it made any difference to the strength of the bond. Had he had an argument with one of his nephews? She felt a clutch of anxiety, remembering the hurtful ways in which her grandfather had lashed out at her in the last few years of his life. In the end she had done them both a disservice by trying to cushion him from reality.

'Rose's blood,' she reminded him. 'They're family, and family naturally like to know what's going on in each other's lives—'

'That's true. So have you told your parents about the extent of the fire?' Peter asked, turning the tables. 'You did say you were going to try to call them?'

'Oh, yes…well…' Emily produced a half-hearted shrug. 'I rang the aid agency head office in Switzerland but they could only promise to try to pass a non-urgent message on. Communications are pretty difficult in that part of Africa at the best of times, and, with the relief teams being constantly on the move, I doubt I'll hear from them any time soon. I just said that there'd been a fire but that I hadn't been hurt. There didn't seem any point banging on about losing the studio. It's pretty small potatoes compared to the grim life-and-death stuff they're handling every day.'

Peter opened his mouth and then closed it again. He had only met her parents once, when they had flown briefly home for James' funeral, and he had been appalled when they had left again almost immediately afterwards to resume their refugee work in Kashmir, barely sparing the time to acknowledge their daughter's grief.

She knew that he didn't think much of Trish and Alan for abandoning their seven-year-old child with Alan's parents so that they could roam the world as humanitarian aid workers. But Emily had preferred the settled existence with her grandparents to the constant travel, hardship and deprivation that her parents embraced with self-sacrificing fervour.

'Anyway, it's not as if they could do anything from where they are,' she said matter-of-factly. 'I was the one who inherited the house and business, so they have no legal responsibilities to uphold...'

Only an emotional one—to their daughter—Peter could have said, but kindly didn't, happily assuming the supportive role he'd assigned himself since her grandfather had died. 'Let's go and have that cup of tea.'

The muffins were as splendid as everything else that came out of Mrs Cooper's oven and after tea in the sun-filled blue and white lounge Emily tried again to express both her thanks and discomfort over his largesse.

'As you said, your parents aren't in a position to help you, but I can,' Peter said, brushing aside her attempts to discuss payment for the materials he had bought.

Unfortunately, with few savings in the bank and all her plans dependent on the insurance report, she could only offer an alternative to cash.

'If I was in trouble I know you'd rush to help in any way you could. In fact you did—you kept coming around to cheer me up in the months after Rose died, when all the other sympathy visits had dwindled, encouraging me to take an interest in something other than my own misery. I'd be a poor friend if I didn't return the favour, wouldn't I?

'Tell her not to be so stubborn, Coop,' he appealed to his housekeeper, who had come to clear away the cups and crumbs. 'Emily's upset over how much my surprise must have cost, and is trying to persuade me that she should work on Rose's wish-list for nothing in order to reimburse me for outfitting a studio for her to do it in. Seems to think I'm being a silly old duffer. I say she shouldn't look a gift horse in the mouth.'

Emily flushed with discomfort as she thanked Mrs Cooper for the delicious muffins and helped place the delicate bone china on the tray.

'I don't think it's silly. I'm incredibly grateful...but it just seems like I'm being paid twice,' she defended herself awkwardly, and caught a glimmer of surprise and cautious approval in the beady black eyes as the older woman straightened.

'I think you might find someone else more stubborn than you,' Mrs Cooper commented, jerking her head at her employer. 'The silly old duffer there is well nigh impossible to budge once he makes up his mind about something. He's been a right dictator over that studio, and pestering me about getting your rooms ready, as if I don't keep every room in this house immaculate—'

'My rooms?' Emily blurted, looking from one to the other in bewilderment. 'What rooms?'

Peter sat forward in his chair, scowling at his housekeeper, who looked grimly satisfied with the results of her remark. 'Now you've gone and spoiled my other surprise. I know that you won't accept any outright financial help from me, Emily, but I thought that you might like to stay here until your affairs were settled and you could find a rental or go back to your own house.'

'But I already have a place to stay—with my friend Julie,' she reminded him.

'Yes, but you said she and her flatmate only have a little two-bedroom flat and you're sleeping on the living-room couch. And you said their boyfriends often stay over, which must make it even more cramped...'

'I don't mind, really,' insisted Emily. 'It's only a temporary arrangement—'

'You don't know how long it might be. And it's right on the other side of Auckland—that's a long way to travel here to work every day. Without a car you'd have to get a train or bus into the central terminal and then another one out here, and buses up this way aren't too frequent...'

And she had turned down a chauffeur-driven Rolls! 'I'm sure I'll get used to it,' she said weakly.

'What you're used to is working from home, with the freedom to come and go from your studio whenever you like,' he said with irrefutable logic. 'You could do that here—I have tons of spare space so we won't get in each other's way.'

She opened her mouth and he held up a stemming hand. 'Before you say no, why don't you let Coop show you your bedroom? It's in the east corner, right across from the garage, and has a separate entrance so you can take a short cut to work!'

Mrs Cooper had mellowed somewhat as she showed a reluctant Emily the luxurious white bedroom and small sitting room next door to the familiar, quiet room where glass-fronted antique cabinets and lacquered oriental tables displayed Rose's neatly labelled Meissen figurines and tableware and her later collection of Chinese blue and white porcelain.

'It's lovely and I don't want to offend Mr Nash, but I think I'm better staying on with my friend,' Emily murmured, enviously fingering the shimmering, silk-embroidered duvet cover. The wide single bed looked so soft and inviting after the hard, uneven foam cushions of Julie's couch she was tempted to fling herself down to see if it felt as good as it looked, but then she might find it even harder to resist temptation. Particularly in the company of a half set of richly decorated players from the famous Meissen Monkey Orchestra, which were playfully arranged in silent duets and trios around the room.

'Thanks for doing all this, though,' she said, waving a hand to include the vase of bright flowers on the mirrored dressing table, the thick, fluffy towels folded on the end of the bed, and the footed bowl of fresh fruit on the coffee table in the sitting room. There was even a basket of packaged feminine toiletries beside the telephone on the bedside table.

'Mr Nash's orders,' the housekeeper shrugged. No wonder she had received such a cool reception at the door, thought Emily, giving the room one last, wistful look. Mrs Cooper must have assumed she had known all about this—perhaps even suspected her of asking for it, or manipulating Peter into offering. She must have been worried that Emily was turning into a freeloader, taking advantage of an old man's compassion.

'Well, thanks anyway—I saw a few necessities there that definitely wouldn't have occurred to a man!'

'Every woman can do with a little hand cream,' said Mrs Cooper primly and the two women exchanged a secret look of understanding.

'So, have you seen enough to make you change your mind?' Peter Nash appeared at the door, rubbing his bony hands together in confident anticipation of a positive answer.

'Ah…' Emily hated to disappoint him, but knew that she had already accepted enough of his generosity.

Mrs Cooper gave her an encouraging nod and discreetly abstracted herself.

Peter, as Emily had feared, did not accept her decision easily and when financial logic and claims of artistic patronage didn't carry his argument, sighed and looked nostalgically around the room.

'This was Rose's favourite part of the house after she got sick. She liked being near her plates, and she used to sit over there in her easy chair by the French doors, basking in the sun, reading her books and magazines, and marking a wish-list off her auction pamphlets. She swore those blessed monkeys used to play her a jig whenever she started to nod off. Looking at them always made her smile.'

'Peter—' Emily's faltering words were cut off by a sudden whomping clatter that made them both move over to the French doors. Hundreds of blooms in the terraced rose gardens along the back of the house whipped their heads in a mad swirl of multi-coloured petals as a yellow helicopter swooped down over the house. It angled around until its cockpit faced the house, hovering like a giant, angry butterfly over the flat circle of tarmac behind the swimming pool at the bottom of the gardens before sinking down on its landing struts with a gentle bounce.

'Looks like you have another visitor,' murmured Emily as the rotors slowed to a stop and the pilot finished flicking switches, opened the door and jumped out, his cropped dark hair firing with glints of red in the strong morning sunlight. He reached to pull a bag and suit-carrier out from the passenger compartment and jogged easily around the wrought-iron pool fence, taking the wide, flagstoned steps between the ranks of terraced roses two at a time.

'And he seems to be in a hurry…'

The tall figure was dressed in a suit but moved with the loose, loping grace of a born athlete confident of his own strength, head down, the long legs powering up the steps with a smooth unbroken rhythm.

'It's Ethan,' said Peter, looking over her shoulder. 'He's always in a hurry. I wonder what he wants?'

'You weren't expecting him?' Emily asked, frowning at the top of the dark head and the glimpse of wraparound sunglasses masking the upper part of his face, aware of something vaguely familiar in the set of the broad shoulders. Just as he lifted his gaze to the house he vanished behind the riot of climbing roses on trellised arches leading to the terrace that ran along the back of the house.

'No,' Peter murmured. 'He usually calls ahead to let me know…for Coop's sake as much as mine. I wonder where he's come from this time?'

Emily knew that Ethan West had been a structural engineer before he had ventured into the rarefied world of custom-built, luxury homes, and that his speciality was building on difficult sites in remote areas of New Zealand.

'When you said he made flying visits, I didn't think you meant literally,' she said, turning away from the window. Ethan's primary home was on Waiheke Island so she supposed it would make sense for him to commute by air to his offices in uptown Auckland when the car or passenger-ferry services didn't fit in with his business schedule. It would only be a fifteen minute flight from the small island out in the Hauraki Gulf to Peter's hilltop home, and only another short hop to the city centre.

'Well, while you see to your nephew I'd better get on with organising myself. I'll just put a box of a few work things I hope I can salvage into the studio, and then I'll unload my personal stuff into the storage locker you asked Jeff to empty for me in the garage. I'll have to make another run to the house because there were a few other boxes that I couldn't manage to squeeze in on this trip, then I'll need to get the car back to Julie, so I won't actually be able to start work in the studio until tomorrow...' As soon as she had picked herself up some bus timetables. The list of things she had to do in order to rebuild her life seemed to be getting longer rather than shorter.

'Oh, but you can't rush off without saying hello to Ethan,' said Peter, clasping her shoulder. 'It's about time I introduced you two...'

Emily looked at him. 'I rather got the impression that you preferred me not to meet your family,' she said quietly. She couldn't have failed to notice that her invitations had never coincided with his nephews' visits or any other guests, and that he had never suggested that they should.

His fingers tightened on her shoulder, his eyes shifting guiltily. 'You can blame that on an old man's selfishness in wanting to keep all your attention for himself,' he said gruffly. 'Is that why you won't accept my invitation to stay—because you think I'm ashamed of our friendship?'

'No, of *course* not—' she hastened to reassure him.

'Then you'll think about it?'

She sighed. 'I'll think about it,' she temporised.

'Because it would mean a great deal to me. *You* mean a lot to me,' he said, his brown eyes gravely intent. 'Just having you around the place has been better than any tonic. You're easy to talk to, not like a lot of young people who are always rush, rush, rush—off with the old and on with the new! And you know that there's no one else I'd trust to spruce up Rose's favourite things. So never, never think you're not valued and wanted, Emily.'

Not quite sure what had prompted his uncharacteristic emotional frankness, Emily felt a warning prickle in her eyes. Since the fire, her own emotions had been riding dangerously close to the surface. She had received plenty of sympathy and commiseration, but there was no substitute for the intimate concern of family. She had never missed her grandfather more than she had this week, as Peter had obviously realised. Impulsively she flung her arms around his gaunt frame and gave him a fierce hug, rising on tiptoe to give his leathery cheek a kiss that made him blush.

'I love you, too!' she said cheekily, blinking away the threat of tears to experience a horrifying sense of *déjà vu* as her gaze met with a lethal pair of blue eyes surveying them from the doorway.

'Should I have knocked?'

They sprang apart, Emily's knees so weak she staggered drunkenly and subsided abruptly onto the bed, while Peter spun around, his blush deepening as he straightened his bow-tie over his bobbing Adam's apple, a spurious picture of guilt.

'Ethan, my boy!' said Peter heartily. 'I was just suggesting to Emily she come out and be introduced.'

'Out of the bedroom?' Dark, arched eyebrows shot up towards a severe widow's peak, a mocking counterpoint to the aridly dry voice. His narrowed eyes swept the room, lingering briefly on each group of simian players. Was he checking that they were all still there?

Oh, God, it *was* him. This wasn't just her over-stressed brain playing morbid tricks on her; there was no mistaking that stony visage and coruscating look.

Peter's eldest nephew was her contemptuous saviour—the Black Knight from the Webbers' party. The man she had taunted and teased like a cheap tart!

He had recognised her, too, the instant that he had seen her peering at him over Peter's shoulder. For a moment she had seen an explosion of disbelief followed by microsecond bursts of puzzlement, confusion and anger.

He had switched to studying his uncle's thin frame with a suppressed intensity. 'I just got back from the South Island yesterday,' he said abruptly. 'When I rang you were out, but Mrs

Cooper was full of your exciting doings on behalf of your young, homeless friend…'

He made her sound like a bag lady, thought Emily hysterically—which, technically at the moment, she supposed she was! Considering Peter's habit of keeping his own counsel, she couldn't really blame the housekeeper for feeling the need to offload her suspicions onto someone whom she knew for certain would have her employer's best interests at heart.

'Coop never knows quite as much as she thinks she does,' retorted Peter, having recovered from his unaccustomed start. 'Emily…?' He reached for her limp hand and drew her to her feet. Miraculously her woolly knees managed to weave themselves some strength and she moved stiff-legged to meet her fate. 'This is my nephew Ethan,' he pronounced with a redundant flourish. 'Ethan, I'd like you to meet Emily Quest, who's become a good friend to me in the last couple of years—as well as doing some finely skilled work. She's a very talented restorer of antique ceramics.'

'Is she indeed?' There was the faintest hiss of acid in his slow sibilance.

Emily's cold hand was completely swallowed by the fiery warmth of a large, slightly abrasive palm, the slow wrap of hard fingers around her delicate bones reminding her with a sinful jolt of the last time they had touched.

'I'm absolutely *fascinated* to meet you, Emily Quest,' he drawled with caustic enthusiasm, his hand tightening by menacing degrees, rendering her effectively his captive. 'I have no doubt that you're *extremely* talented at…whatever it is you do.'

Emily bit her lip and struggled to pull the corners of her mouth into the semblance of a polite smile. 'Hello, Ethan. Peter has talked a lot about you—'

She gave his hand a firm shake, pulling her elbow back with a vigorous jerk, feeling a complete fool when he let her fingers slide easily through his, as if he had never intended anything else.

'How curious—he hasn't talked at all about *you*. What do you suppose that means?'

'Perhaps he didn't consider me worth mentioning until now.' She shrugged.

'Such modesty!' He cocked his head and took his time looking her over, from her tousled head to her curling toes inside the white socks. 'You know, I get the strangest feeling that you're familiar to me in some indefinable way,' he mused. 'I'm sure if I think about it long enough I'll work out why…'

Peter tensed, as if he had only just become aware of the strange undercurrents. 'You're imagining things—'

'Actually, he's not,' said Emily, tired of waiting for the axe to fall. 'Ethan and I *have* seen each other before—at a party a couple of years ago. A rather wild party I don't think either of us ended up enjoying very much. I behaved badly and flirted with him, and Ethan turned me down flat.'

There was a small silence, then he smiled. A rock with teeth.

'That's not the way I remember it,' he said.

And Emily's heart sank into her cotton socks.

CHAPTER THREE

PETER LOOKED FROM his nephew's white smile to Emily's embarrassed face with a puzzled expression, halfway between delight and dismay.

'So I didn't really have to introduce you two at all,' he realised, sounding disappointed.

'Actually, you did. Emily and I never got around to exchanging names…' Ethan trailed off suggestively, still holding Emily's apprehensive gaze.

A graphic vision of the way she had taunted him that night popped into her head, and she could feel a wave of heat creeping up the back of her neck. Talk about your sins coming back to haunt you!

This time she had no bold mask of make-up to hide behind. Most of her cosmetics were still in the bathroom directly above her burnt-out studio, roped off as potentially at risk of collapse; the rest were now bundled in a plastic bag buried somewhere in the boot of the car. Today all she had on her face was some of Julie's sun-blocking foundation, which was a shade too dark for her skin tone, and a dash of nude lipstick. Even though she didn't usually wear make-up at work, for fear of contaminating the delicate materials she was handling, she had felt she needed a little feminine boost this morning, when setting out to grub amongst the ashes of her former life.

'It wasn't the kind of party that encouraged formal introductions,' said Emily. 'The music was so loud it was difficult to think, let alone hear what people were saying.'

Except in that quiet, back room, she could see Ethan West thinking, but he didn't say anything to contradict her words. He didn't call her a liar, or accuse her of being a thief, but instead of relief she felt her anxiety burrow deeper.

'Oh, I see,' said Peter, although, thankfully, he didn't—the faintly troubled frown lifting from his lined forehead. 'So that's why you never mentioned anything about knowing Ethan when I talked to you about him.'

'As far as I was concerned I didn't know him.' Emily was emphatic.

'You mean you didn't know that you knew me,' Ethan pointed out with infuriating pedantry.

'I didn't know you at all,' she reiterated.

'Not in the biblical sense, anyway,' he said. 'Although not for want of trying.'

'It isn't as if you have any family photos on display around here, other than the ones of Rose in your office.' Emily talked hurriedly over the top of his low comment. 'And I might not have recognised him from a photograph, anyway. It was such a long time ago, and we met so briefly—'

'Yes, I was just another John that night, as far as Emily was concerned—' he paused just long enough to receive her horrified look, before clarifying '—John Doe, I mean. Or should I have said Joe Bloggs?' he mused, cocking another goading eyebrow at her blooming face.

'Oh, ho, I can see how you wouldn't like that.' Peter laughed, completely missing the insulting sexual allusion. 'Ethan's not used to being thought of as just one of the crowd,' he told Emily. 'He's a high achiever—always has been. Even as a kid he used to set himself impossible goals.'

'What happened when he couldn't achieve them?' Emily couldn't help asking.

'Ah, yes, that's the measure of a man, the way he handles

defeat, eh, Ethan?' Peter reached up to clap his nephew on his shoulder. 'As I remember it he never cried. He would just stick out that jaw of his and keep doggedly at it until he succeeded.'

Emily looked up at the iron-hard jaw, and noted a slight nick under the point of his smooth chin. Mr Perfect had cut himself shaving this morning. He had a tiny sprinkle of grey in the dark brown hair, too, she saw as she searched for a few reassuring flaws in his aura of invulnerability, and his skin was surprisingly pale for a man who was such a reputed powerhouse of energy. He wasn't wearing a tie and the two buttons left open on his blue shirt revealed a suspiciously glossy collar-bone. A man who oozed testosterone the way he did would surely have a hairy chest. He must wax, she decided with a disparaging inward sniff. Vain, as well as arrogant.

'So you've never actually failed at anything, then?' she reasoned, managing to imply his character had therefore never been really measured.

He gave her his patented, menacing, ice-chip stare. 'Not if it was something I really, really wanted.'

As he really, really wanted her out of his uncle's life?

'I bet you were fun in the playground,' she muttered.

'I always fought fair.'

'You only punch your own weight?' she shot swiftly back. 'That's good to know.'

His gaze sank down to the tee shirt shrouding her slightly over-abundant curves and lingered, as if he was mentally weighing her breasts. She felt them tingle in response to the mocking male scrutiny and hurriedly folded her arms, crushing the burgeoning tips into obedient submission. His eyes merely moved on to the ripe swell of her hips below the hem of her tee shirt and the straining side-seams of her jeans.

Her arms tightened, fists clenching against the sides of her breasts, unconsciously plumping them forward as she smouldered impotently under his inspection. Beneath his broad shoulders he was lean and slim-hipped, but, damn it, he was at least six feet two—he had to weigh more than she did!

'Women naturally have more body-fat than men,' she heard herself blurting out. 'But muscle is heavier.'

One muscle in particular. The wayward thought popped into her head as his eyes rose back to her face, and she only just stopped herself looking down at the front of his light grey trousers. What was it about the man that made her want to act like the brazen hussy he thought her to be?

'I guess size is relative, isn't it?' he responded. 'Experience is the great leveller. Size doesn't always succeed over rat-cunning.'

'Especially if the rat is over six feet tall,' Emily agreed sweetly.

'Brute force backed with intelligence is always a winner,' he purred.

Peter's head had been going back and forth. 'What are you two talking about?' he said in confusion.

'We're reminiscing,' his nephew said.

'About the party? Where was it, anyway?' Peter asked.

'Your friends, the Webbers'.'

'Not friends—acquaintances. Sean Webber just happened to go to some of the same auctions as Rose. I suppose that's why you were there, Emily. You did a bit of work on a few of Sean's Chinese pieces a few years ago, didn't you? On Rose's recommendation…'

This was dangerous ground. 'Quest Restorations did,' said Emily carefully, aware of Ethan West's sudden alertness.

Fortunately, Peter was already rolling on: 'I never took to Sean. A real snob. Thought the fact he inherited his money made him better than those of us who earned it by honest graft,' growled Peter. 'He sucked up to Rose though. Knew she came from an aristocratic background. Didn't matter to Sean that her parents cut her out of their lives when she ran away to marry someone whose alcoholic mother cleaned toilets for a living. In fact Sean probably approved!'

He shook his head. 'I didn't think you liked him either, Ethan. He oiled up to your father in the same way, and yet Malcolm was just as much *persona non grata* with the Wests as Rose when he decided to follow in his big sister's footsteps. I shouldn't have thought you'd give any invitation of Sean's a second look.'

'It was his son's party—and I wasn't there by choice,' Ethan said tersely.

You and me both, thought Emily.

'I was trying to find Dylan.' He shrugged. 'He was doing PR back then for some show Michael was selling. Not that it panned out, after the party trashed the house that night and Michael was hauled off in the police raid. The Webbers had to slam him in three-month rehab to keep it out of the press and try to buy him off some serious drug charges—'

He broke off as he saw Emily gaping at him, her azure-blue eyes wide within their natural frame of mink-brown lashes.

'You didn't get scooped up in that raid, too, did you, Emily?' he said smoothly.

'I-I left early.' She gulped, going hot and cold at the thought of what would have happened if she'd been arrested and had her bag searched. The flask was the last commission that Quests had executed for Sean Webber, and Emily hadn't wanted to invite trouble by encouraging any further contact.

'So you were safely tucked between the sheets when the main action went down?' From his silky tone it was clear that he thought she was more likely to have been tucked between some man's thighs.

Her eyelids drooped, veiling the fury in her eyes as she recalled the painful reality of the rest of that night, and the anxious days and nights that had followed: the caffeine-and-sugar-fuelled hours of intense concentration she had spent hunched over a magnifying glass in the studio, stripping the flask repair back to its original break and beginning the delicate, painstaking process of cleaning and rebonding.

'Something like that,' she said, absently massaging the muscles at the back of her neck where tension tended to gather after prolonged close work.

'Good God!' said Peter. 'You young people do live exciting lives—'

'Not so young in my case—but surely you can't be older than thirty,' Ethan said to Emily.

'I'm twenty-six,' she snapped, and saw from his smirk that she had reacted precisely as expected to the dangled insult. Why couldn't he have asked if he had wanted to know her age?

'I hope you found Dylan before he fell into mischief,' Peter continued.

'Dylan doesn't fall, he jumps,' said Ethan drily. 'As it turned out Michael had lent him the Webbers' Ferrari to take a girl out for a spin around town. Luckily I was able to get the cops to pick him up for me.'

His own *brother?* 'Wasn't that a bit extreme?' said Emily, shaken at this evidence of his ruthlessness. Even Peter looked taken aback.

'It was a night of extremes,' Ethan commented, more truly than he knew, his deep voice gentling in a way that wrapped around Emily's senses as he said to his uncle, 'It was the night that you called me from the hospital to say that Aunt Rose had suddenly deteriorated, and was being transferred to the hospice.'

Peter blinked, remembering. 'That's right…and she died just a couple of days later.' He smiled sadly. 'I remember you and Dylan turning up at some ungodly hour to sit with us and talk… you in a fancy black tie because you'd been at some swanky opening—how Rose loved that… That was the same night?'

Ethan nodded. 'The tail-end of it, anyway.'

'Oh, God,' murmured Emily, impulsively putting her hand on his forearm. 'I'm so sorry,' she said on a surge of empathy. No wonder he had been so granite-faced at the party, impatient with the noisy frivolity and contemptuous of the self-destructive behaviour on display, when he had known that his aunt was having to fight for every precious extra moment of life. He must have been deeply worried and every bit as intent on his completing his mission as Emily had been on hers. And she had chosen that moment to prowl up to him like a cat in heat!

He looked down at her hand lying against the lightweight

wool of his jacket. It was as contradictory as everything else about her so far—delicate yet strong, soft yet not pampered, the fingers scattered with tiny, old scars, the short, unpainted nails all symmetrical and obviously cared for, but rimmed with black grime. Not the hands of a typical vamp. And yet…

'How awful for you,' she was gushing. 'If I'd known—' she stumbled to a halt as his hand clamped over hers, his ruthless mouth denting with a sardonic twist.

'You would have…what? Offered me comfort?' He turned aside from his uncle and lowered his voice for her ears only. 'A soft bosom to cry on?' His arm was like iron under her crushed fingers. He obviously didn't need or want her sympathy. 'You didn't seem like the kind of woman who was looking for the sensitive side of a man.'

'Oh, what did you think I was looking for?' she said, realising it had been a mistake to touch him, for it intensified her over-awareness of his innate masculinity.

His eyes glinted through his lashes, which were every bit as lush as her own.

'Discipline.'

Her nude mouth rounded into a shocked 'O', her eyes shading to an outrageous blue as her creative imagination leapt into overdrive. Visualising herself at the mercy of his strict sexual discipline was wickedly arousing. He would relish giving the orders in bed, and demand her eager compliance to his every whim. Her fingers involuntarily contracted, digging into his sleeve as she tried in vain to dampen down her forbidden fantasies.

Perhaps he had just meant that she needed to learn to behave properly in public, she told herself sternly… Or perhaps not, she thought, seeing the fiendish satisfaction in his gleaming eyes as he watched her suffer her hot flush. He had expected her to leap to precisely the conclusion she had, proving to himself, no doubt, that she was no innocent where sex was concerned.

Nor *was* she—but her sexual experience was restricted to the exploratory fumblings of a young boy and the shattering manipulations of a smooth-talking con man, and in the last two years she had been far too busy caring and then mourning for her grandfather and trying to keep the business afloat to worry about her exercising her libido. In truth, she had never found anything that could quite match the intense physical awe and exhilaration she had felt when she had been allowed to handle an exquisite piece of rare, Chinese porcelain that had survived over four hundred years of continuous human ownership!

She tried to pull her hand free, but this time Ethan wasn't co-operating and rather than get involved in a losing scuffle she just lifted her chin and gave him a disdainful look out of her faintly up-tilted eyes.

'Well, whatever the unwelcome circumstances of your meeting the first time round, this has turned out to be a happy coincidence, hasn't it?' Peter inserted blithely into their unspoken war of words.

Emily had another name for it.

'Telephone call for you, Mr Nash!' The housekeeper's sing-song call echoed along the hallway.

'I thought I'd switched the answer machine on.' Peter frowned. He popped his head out the door. 'Take a message for me, will you?'

'It's Mr Robinson, from the lawyers'—he says he's just answering your call. Do you still want me to deal with it?' came the crusty reply.

'Oh!' Peter's shoulders stiffened and he hesitated for a moment before swinging around, a nervous smile twitching at his mouth as he deliberately avoided his nephew's gaze and spoke to Emily: 'Look, I really need to take this, my dear… Why don't you and Ethan go and have a chat in the lounge where it's more comfortable? I shouldn't be too long.' His smile brightened as he continued in a rush: 'Or, better still, go and sit out in the sun on the verandah and enjoy the view, and I'll send Coop out with another plate of muffins—with a black coffee for you, of course, Ethan, I know how you like to swim in the stuff…'

In other words, he didn't want to risk them wandering within earshot of his telephone call, thought Emily as he limped hastily away.

Ethan was obviously thinking the same thing. 'What's he suddenly want with the family lawyer?' he murmured, pinning Emily with a suspicious look.

'How should I know? It's none of my business,' she told him, trying another fruitless tug of her arm.

'Isn't it? You seem to have made quite a business of cosying up to him, *my dear.*' His cruel mimicry dripped with menace. 'Perhaps because you can see some profit in it…'

She threw back her head and glared at him. 'I don't like what you're suggesting—'

'Neither do I.' His voice bristled with hostility. 'I don't like the idea that you're targeting a vulnerable old man behind his family's back.'

'I don't know what you're talking about,' she said, immediately on the defensive.

He pulled her closer as she tried to lean away from his accusing face. 'You've persuaded him to spend a large amount of money on this so-called studio for you already, according to Mrs C—'

'I didn't, your uncle did it as a surprise, out of the goodness of his heart,' she protested stoutly, remembrance of her own misgivings leaking into her voice, spurring his predatory suspicion.

'Rather a big surprise from someone who's always been extremely cautious with his money. Uncle Peter was never big into charity before—'

'It's not charity,' she flared as he pressed on the open wound. 'I'm going to be doing my restoration work here. I did offer to pay him back—'

'And I'll bet he refused,' he guessed shrewdly.

'Out of compassion for my situation,' she said through gritted teeth. 'Mrs Cooper must have mentioned the fire—'

'Ah, yes, your big sob story…'

'It's not a story. It *happened*—it even made the news, for

goodness sake. Look it up if you want to! And as a *friend*, Peter offered to help me out.'

'And of course you couldn't refuse your very generous new friend—or should we call him a benefactor?'

'Not so new. We've known each other for a few years—'

'Strange that I didn't see you at Rose's funeral, then.'

'I—we—unfortunately, I couldn't be there,' she said, faltering under the battery of his focused aggression. 'My grandfather was very ill at the time—'

'Not so ill that you couldn't take time off to play party-girl a few days before.'

'He had a fall,' was all she said, lifting her chin, refusing to dignify his slur with a more comprehensive explanation of the infirmities that had made James Quest's last few years of life increasingly difficult for both of them. 'Grandfather and I sent a card, and flowers. Peter understood. And later, I came to visit…'

'And started to worm your way into his confidence.'

'It wasn't like that.' Under pressure of his controlling hand she gripped his arm and squeezed. It made no more impression than if she had been pressing an iron bar. 'Would you mind letting go of my hand, now, please?'

'Why, what do you want to do with it?' he goaded, her polite dignity only seeming to infuriate him even further.

'Don't tempt me,' she said, eyeing his arrogant cheekbone.

'Why not? Are you that easy to distract, Miss Quest?' he mocked. 'Are you starting to think I might be a more attractive proposition than my uncle? I'm just as rich, and I'm certainly more capable of giving you a run for my money in bed.'

'Don't be disgusting! I told you, we're just friends.'

'So how come he's never mentioned this so-called friendship before? I spoke to Dylan on the way over here, and he said he'd never met you, either. If this relationship is so innocent, why has Peter been hiding you like some dirty little secret?'

'I don't know!' she cried. 'Maybe because he knows what a suspicious and narrow-minded beast you are!'

'Is it narrow-minded to be worried when I find my elderly uncle hugging and kissing in the bedroom with a sexy young babe with big blue eyes and even bigger b—'

'How dare you?' she spluttered, cutting him off before he could complete the crude remark, while her emotions see-sawed between anger and disbelief. Babe? Sexy? How could he think she was sexy in a baggy shirt, ash-clogged hair and no make-up? She didn't know whether to laugh or cry. She would obviously never shake that first image he had of her in the fishnet tights and skimpy lace dress.

'Are you denying it?'

What? Being young, having big blue eyes and breasts that were larger than average—or being sexy? she wondered in wild confusion, then realised he had meant the hugging and kissing.

'We—I—' But it was too late; he was taking her brief moment of honest bewilderment as a clear admission of guilt. With a rough exclamation of angry disgust he dropped her arm as if it were contaminated, but freedom was no longer her prime concern and, although she edged to the door, she didn't leave. She couldn't, not with her professional as well as personal reputation at stake.

It wouldn't do for him to go rampaging off to spew his vile allegations in front of anyone else. Poor Peter would be shocked, embarrassed and hurt—not only at the suggestion that he was her sugar daddy, but at the implication that he was being played for a fool. She knew from bitter experience how sensitive an old man's pride could be to any hint of incompetence. If he was confronted about it, his relationship with his nephew might be irretrievably damaged, and the innocent pleasure he took in Emily's companionship for ever tainted. For Peter's sake, as well as her own, she at least had to make an *effort* to explain, even if she had little confidence in making any headway against Ethan's determined prejudice.

'Look,' she said, choking back her resentment and drawing on the deep well of patience that made her so good at her job, 'your uncle and I enjoy talking together, that's *all*. He's been tremendously kind. What you saw—it was completely innocent—a casual expression of gratitude that you misinterpreted…'

His cruel mouth tightened, and she instantly comprehended her mistake. Pointing out that the onus for the whole nasty situation was on him was not likely to placate his arrogant self-certainty.

Sure enough, he was quick to slip the blade in: 'What was it I heard you saying to Peter? "I love you, too"…' he quoted in a sticky-sweet, velvet-dark drawl that caressed her senses and jolted her into wondering what it would feel like to hear him say the words with ardent sincerity.

Don't even go there, Emily!

'That's hardly something that can be misinterpreted; unless, of course, you were lying—just saying what you thought he wanted to hear,' he added with that corrosive cynicism she so disliked.

'You're taking it out of context,' she said, holding gamely onto her temper in the face of his intransigence. She felt a very strong affection for Peter, but it was demeaning to both of them to be forced to quantify it. 'I'm sorry if you got the wrong impression, but I can assure you that you certainly did.' Eyeing his dangerously attractive face, she felt a rush of nervous apprehension, and it suddenly seemed imperative to get him out of the bedroom. 'Perhaps you might feel more inclined to listen over your cup of coffee…'

She turned to lead the way, but his hand shot out to slam flat against the door jamb, creating a sloping barrier with his braced arm that she would have to be a limbo dancer to evade.

'Exactly what—is—your—game?' he demanded softly in her ear, seeming more suspicious than ever at her conciliatory manner.

She backed her shoulders to the smooth face of the open door, shaking her head, her cropped curls bouncing in sharp denial. 'I don't play games.'

His face tautened with predatory triumph. 'Oh, Emily, we both know that for a damned lie!'

He lifted a hand suddenly towards her face and she flinched, hitting the back of her head against the polished wood.

'Ouch!'

His eyes darkened to grey steel as his hand continued its threatening rise until his middle finger touched the smooth skin above her left eyebrow. He rubbed firmly and drew it away again, revealing the blackened swirl of his fingerprint to her tear-stung eyes.

'You had a black speck on your face,' he said, erasing the smudge with a roll of his finger and thumb. 'It fell out of your hair when you shook your head.'

'It must be soot,' she said, whisking at the place he had touched, which was now tingling as if the fleck of carbon had been a live ember. 'I've been at my house this morning. The house that *burned down*,' she emphasised. She rubbed at the tender spot on the back of her head. 'Ouch!'

'You shouldn't have been so skittish. What did you think I was going to do?' he asked, showing his first thread of genuine amusement—at her expense.

'Oh, I don't know, you had cold blue murder in your eyes… throttle me, perhaps?' she tossed at him with furious sarcasm.

'How very mundane of me. And stuff your body where?' he asked drily.

Her eyes fell on the bed beyond him and she blushed. His glance tracked hers and his eyebrows rose as he looked back at her with a tormenting smile.

'Under the bed…or in it?' His silky question brought more blood scorching to her face. 'Is that one of the sex games you like to play? To be throttled by your lover? I understand it can intensify an orgasm to an addictive degree.'

'I never— That's— You have a very perverted mind.' Emily gasped, scrubbing harder at her head to get rid of the invasive image of Ethan West lying on top of her on the white bed, his big hands wrapped around her, holding her down while his nude body thrust relentlessly between her thighs, driving her to intense completion.

'And you don't? You're blushing like a Deep Secret.'

'I don't have any deep secrets,' Emily lied, disorientated by his further descent into the realms of bizarre.

'It's a hybrid tea rose,' he explained, his eyes on her blooming cheeks, 'one of the darkest of all the reds.'

'Oh…' While she grappled with the mind-boggling idea of this stone-hard man knowing anything about flowers, he leaned forward, one arm still braced across the doorway, the other sliding around to the nape of her neck.

'You're going to bruise yourself doing that. Let me see what you've done to yourself…'

'No, I—'

He was already cupping the back of her skull with his large hand, fingers sliding through her fine hair, probing for the bump.

Her shoulders squirmed against the smooth surface of the door. 'I don't need you to—'

'Be still!' he said coolly.

Her small nostrils flared. 'Don't give me orders—'

'Then stop acting like a child.'

'First I'm a *femme fatale* and now I'm a child. Make up your mind!' she snapped.

'Oh, I will,' he promised, with such ominous certainty she shivered, and covered it with another complaint.

'Ouch!'

'Don't fuss. It's only a tiny bump.' His hand came back to rest on the back of her neck, his fingers firm on the sensitive skin above the neck of her tee shirt.

'I know, that's why I didn't need you touching me!'

The fierce statement prompted a crackling little pause.

'Does my touch disturb you that much?' His thumb began to describe little circles on the downy skin in the hollow at her nape.

'No,' she answered quickly. Too quickly, judging by the diabolical light that leapt into his eyes, turning them to hot ice.

'Oh, really? Shall we put that to the test?'

He jerked her into his arms, crushing her breasts against his hard chest, the arm that was barring the door swinging down to catch her around the hips, pressing her into the potent heat of his braced thighs, the hand at the back of her neck holding her still for his swooping mouth.

Simmering tension exploded into a firestorm of furious elation. His hard lips devoured her strangled cry, feeding on the shocked excitement that shuddered through her body as his tongue thrust past her teeth to delve into the rich, creamy-wet depths of her captive mouth. The taste of him was tart and spicy, a tantalising burst of exotic flavour on her tongue that made her hungry for more. The musky natural scent of his warm skin with its underlying hint of soap and citrus filled her nostrils, the hard angles of his face blurring as her eyelids fluttered down, blocking out everything but the on-rushing tide of hot, syrupy pleasure.

Some vague, still-sane part of her brain warned her that his angry intent was to insult and demean, but somehow the message got tangled up in the transmission and, instead of pushing against his powerful shoulders, her fingers clenched the open lapels of his jacket as she rode out the storm of fiery sensation, dragging herself deeper into the ravishment of his plundering kiss.

His big hand swept down over the rounded cheeks of her bottom confined in the taut denim, adjusting her more tightly against the sinewy flex of his thighs, then slipped under the loose hem of her tee shirt. His fingers skimmed swiftly up the side of her ribcage to trace the smooth underwire of her lacy bra around to the tiny satin bow that nestled in her generous cleavage.

Electric shivers goosed her skin at his trailing touch and her jaw tensed, her teeth involuntarily testing the firm resilience of his limber tongue. He responded instantly with a few sensuous nips of his own, a deep, growling rumble in his chest vibrating through the crushed tips of her breasts.

'Don't pretend you don't want this,' he warned savagely, shifting his stance so that he could palm the fullness of one breast, his fingers spreading to accommodate the lush ripeness overflowing the lace cup and contracting to massage the swollen flesh, drawing a ragged whimper from her love-bitten lips.

'Oh, yes…' he taunted with raw satisfaction as his probing thumb found the betraying outline of her lace-encased nipple and scraped a circle around the rigid little knot, 'you like what I'm doing to you, don't you, Emily?' he demanded, lifting his marauding mouth so that he could look down at her dazed blue eyes, the hand behind her neck controlling her feeble attempt to reclaim her disordered senses. 'My touch more than disturbs you—you're such a hot little piece, I could have you right here and now—all I have to do is this…' He pinched at the painfully engorged nipple, playing with it between his fingers, at the same time bending down to run his hot tongue around her glistening lips, making a rough sound of triumph as he felt her arching shudder of helpless response.

'No…' In spite of her fainting excitement she managed to gasp a thready objection to his gloating words, but it only served to spur him on to an even more devastating demonstration of sexual mastery.

His mouth slanted over hers and burrowed again into the dark depths, suckling on her tongue in hot, strong bursts, keeping rhythmic pace with the milking movements of his fingers as they thrust beneath the cup of her bra and fondled her naked breast and velvety nipple with taunting skill.

He pushed his thigh between her legs, his virile hardness rubbing against the damp notch of her jeans.

'Are you like this with everyone or is it just me?' he said in a gravelly whisper that flayed her to the bone. 'If you want me to give you what you're panting for, you'll have to rethink your strategy with Peter. I don't think he would feel so beneficent if he walked in right now…'

From somewhere Emily found the strength and the will to rip herself away from his torrid embrace.

She staggered back, wiping the back of her forearm and hand across her mouth to rid herself of the bitter taste of self-betrayal. To think that she had actually believed that he might be feeling the same thrill of discovery that she had experienced! Her face tightened with revulsion at her own gullibility.

To her disbelief her gesture appeared to offend him. 'Don't do that.' He prowled after her, bristling with outraged masculinity.

'Do what? This?' Her scalded hurt boiled to the surface and she continued to back away, boldly repeating the action, drawing her arm with taunting slowness across her throbbing mouth, her eyes glowing with electric-blue defiance. To make sure he got the message she mimed a spitting action with her tongue and almost choked as he made a sudden lunge and grabbed her shoulders, snatching her back against his chest.

'I told you not to do that,' he growled, sealing his mouth down over hers in another soul-stirring kiss, taking his time over the sensual punishment, not stopping until they were both panting.

His eyes were pure steel, burnished with brutal satisfaction as they shafted her with a knowing look. 'I warned you! If you do it again, I'll know exactly what it is you're asking for...' He paused, as if expecting another act of defiance, and when it didn't come he scowled, reluctantly letting her go. 'Don't think because you can wind my uncle around your little finger that you have any chance of getting me to dance to your tune.'

She rallied to the ridiculous charge, lifting her chin.

'You're starting to mix your metaphors, Ethan. I thought you were supposed to be a civilised, well-educated man but it seems reports of your intelligence have been over-inflated—much like your puffed-up ego!'

Some day soon he was going to rue his reckless words, and she was going to make him grovel in the dirt before she accepted his apology. *If* she accepted it at all! she thought, revenge fantasies dancing in her head.

He gave a dark, scornful laugh. 'Peter might have offered to set you up here in your own little studio, but don't think that'll give you free access to his cheque-book—most of his money's tied up in a family trust.'

'Oh, but he's offered me much more than that!' she took great pleasure in informing him. 'Didn't Mrs Cooper warn you that he'd asked me to live here with him as well? That's why he was showing me this bedroom suite…*my* bedroom, now, apparently, so I think I'd be perfectly within my rights to ask *you* to leave…'

He stiffened. 'When I arrived, Coop said that you'd turned him down, that you'd opted for staying with one of your girlfriends—'

'What? Turn down a luxurious lifestyle at a sweet old codger's expense for a lumpy couch in an overcrowded flat? No self-respecting gold-digging slut would be that stupid!' she jeered, beginning to enjoy herself. 'No, it's the life of Riley for me from now on. I'll be breakfasting on champagne and dining on caviar!'

His eyes had narrowed at her shameless gloating. 'This is just a wind-up, isn't it?' She could see his engineer's brain ticking over like a calculator. 'For whatever reason, you *did* refuse. You're not moving in at all—'

'Watch me!' she snapped at him, determined not to give him the satisfaction of being right. 'I was just about to unload my stuff from the car when you came buzzing onto the scene.' She turned on her heel and marched out into the hall.

'Hadn't you better come and drink your coffee before it gets cold?' she bid, emphasising her point by assuming the snooty air of a polite hostess enduring an unwelcome guest in her home.

He followed, festering silently in her wake, but by the time she stepped onto the verandah he had regained her shoulder, and refocused his attack.

'And what if I was to suggest to Peter that he bring in an independent appraiser to view Aunt Rose's collection? Someone who could inspect and revalue it piece by piece, particularly in view of the ongoing restoration process of the last few years?' he asked. 'How would you react to the idea?'

Ah…so he *had*, after all, seen more than she had bargained for that fateful night!

She halted in her tracks and gave a sour laugh. 'I'd tell you to join the queue.'

He was startled into his natural courtesy. 'I beg your pardon?'

She turned, ticking off her fingers. 'I'm being investigated by the insurance company, the fire department, the police, and probably the Inland Revenue Department once they discover my GST returns for the quarter have burnt to a crisp.

'So bring on your appraiser—bring in all the experts you like. I won't even pretend to be insulted, because I'd welcome the chance for vindication in at least one area of my life!'

CHAPTER FOUR

EMILY primly presided over the freshly laid tray on the verandah table, hoping that the shade thrown by the canvas patio umbrella would disguise the slight puffiness she could feel around her tender mouth.

On the other side of the table Ethan West lounged, toying with his coffee, and with Emily's nerves. He, too, was lurking in the shadows rather than the full glare of the sun, but for a different reason. Mrs Cooper, when she had brought out his coffee with a fussiness that bespoke her strong partiality, had chivvied him to scoot his wooden chair under the protection of the umbrella.

'He burns easily,' she had told Emily chattily, handing her the slip-on shoes she had left outside the door, now scrupulously clean; obviously trying to make up for ratting her out.

'Oh, dear,' said Emily, stuffing her feet into the damp shoes, mentally striking a match and setting it to the cuff of his custom-tailored suit.

'Everything around you seems to be dangerously inflammable,' remarked Ethan, shrewdly picking up on her wayward thought as he reefed off his jacket and draped it over the back of his chair. How could he be so perceptive in some respects and so wilfully blind in others? 'Careful you don't get your fingers burnt.'

'They already are,' she said, waggling the shiny pink finger-tips she had acquired when she had unwisely put her hand to a brass door-knob on the night of the fire.

Instead of shooting back another mocking one-liner, he frowned, leaning forward for a closer look. 'Do they hurt?'

'Only when I laugh,' she said flippantly. In truth she had been afraid that she might have permanently lost some of the fine sensitivity in the pads of her fingers, so critical to her work, but, instead, burning off the top few layers of skin had brought the nerves closer to the surface and seemed to have increased her tactile ability.

'Then I hope you've learned your lesson,' he said, settling back in his seat.

'Good girls don't play with fire? And bad boys spoil in the sun!' She was trying hard to picture him as an unattractive boiled lobster. Unfortunately, his devouring kiss had changed everything. There was no getting away from the fact that, no matter how she might loathe and despise him, he was a seriously sexy man.

'It's his skin,' Mrs Cooper chimed in helpfully, putting two muffins onto his plate, and then adding a third for good measure. 'He's very sensitive.'

As sensitive as an elephant!

'I can tell,' Emily cooed. 'He's so wonderfully in touch with his feminine side…'

The bitch part, anyway, her sweetly smiling eyes informed him.

Ethan ran a hand over his cheek and jaw, hiding the reluctant tick at the corners of his mouth as Mrs Cooper retreated into the coolness of the house. 'She means to the effects of the sun,' he clarified. 'I get my susceptibility from my volatile mother. She was a true redhead—in appearance as well as in temperament.'

That explained the fiery sparks in his hair, and the lack of an obvious tan in a man who must spend a fair bit of time outdoors.

Emily knew that his parents had both been killed in a light-plane crash several years ago, but she refused to allow his quirky comment to soften her defences.

'So you inherited a slight trace of one maternal trait, and a big, fat dollop of the other,' she said, leaving him to work out which was which.

'Actually, I'm generally considered to have a cool head and a highly stable personality,' he said wryly. He ruffled a hand over the top of his head, stirring the dark embers. 'But if you want me to prove to you that I'm a natural redhead, I'd be happy to oblige.'

She only just stopped herself from rising to his sly taunt. 'That won't be necessary,' she said repressively.

'Pity.'

'Do you always have to bring everything down to the level of sexual innuendo?' she said, snatching up a muffin she had had no intention of touching, and taking a combative bite.

He looked surprised. 'Was I talking about sex?' he said innocently. 'I thought we were discussing genetics. By proof I was referring to photographs of generations of redheaded Wests. What did you think I meant?'

He selected a muffin off his own plate and took a matching bite, holding her gaze as his straight white teeth sank deep into the sweetly tart concoction.

She swallowed. A tiny, tender spot on her lower lip throbbed at the reminder of his sensuous bite and she unknowingly worried at it with the tip of her tongue, her fingers absently crumbling the rest of her muffin.

Only when his winter-blue eyes became fixed on her mouth did she realise what she was doing, and quickly framed a diversionary question. 'Does your brother have red highlights in his hair, too?'

'Not a trace. He's ash-blond—the spitting image of my father, and he seems to have a very similar philosophy of life.'

'What's that?'

His mouth took on a cynical twist. 'Live fast, die young.'

Emily vaguely remembered something about leaving a good-looking corpse being part of the original quotation, but it wasn't surprising that Ethan had left off the tag-line.

Malcolm West had only been in his mid-forties when he died at the controls of his personal plane, still young by modern standards, but it was not a pretty way to die.

Prior to his death he had won—and lost—several fortunes running cut-price airlines around the South Pacific region, and Emily wondered whether Ethan's granite hardness and suspicious nature were a reaction against the roller-coaster effects of a boom-bust childhood.

'And what's *your* personal philosophy?' she asked, seizing the chance for a further insight into the murky workings of his mind.

But he wasn't co-operating. 'Live slow and die old,' he drawled. He demolished his muffin in two more wolfish bites, washed down with a mouthful of steaming black coffee, and started another.

'What about your parents?' he said, deftly turning the tables. 'Which one do you most resemble?'

The question seemed innocuous enough, but by now Emily was wary of his verbal traps. She reached to pour a glass of iced-water from the pottery jug Mrs Cooper had left sitting in the centre of the table while she decided it was safe to answer.

'Neither, really. They're very tall and fair-haired, and both of them are extremely thin…' she tensed, wishing she hadn't mentioned that little detail, when his gaze drifted with a reminiscent smile to the breasts he had so recently handled '…but that could be the result of over-generosity, rather than genetics,' she finished, unaware of the faint nuance of old guilt that had crept into her voice. 'They're prone to giving away their rations and living off the smell of an oily rag.'

Curiosity brought his eyes winging back to her face, the smirk wiped from his lips.

'Why, where do they live?' he said sharply.

Perhaps he imagined they were starving in some fetid foreign prison, she thought sourly—and that she came from a whole family of con artists.

'Everywhere and nowhere,' she said with deliberate vagueness.

He wasn't going to let her get away with it. He sat up. 'What the hell does that mean?' he rapped out.

No, he certainly didn't like being kept out of the information loop. No wonder he had come hot-footing to investigate his uncle's apparent brainstorm.

'It means they rarely stay long in one place—at the moment, it's somewhere in Central Africa, at one of the missions,' she said, sipping her water.

'Your parents are *missionaries?*' His startled incredulity was her reward.

His coffee cup had rattled on its saucer, and a drop of coffee splashed out onto the tempered-glass table top. She watched in malicious silence as it soaked into the edge of his immaculate French cuff, making an ugly brown blot on the light blue cotton.

For an instant she flirted with the idea of allowing him to believe she was a vicar's daughter, but she was forestalled by Peter's arrival and eager plunge into the conversation.

'Not missionaries, although they do seem to go to the extremes of altruism with a very similar fervour!' he said, explaining their demanding jobs as he carefully negotiated the single step and limped out onto the timber decking. He always insisted that it didn't bother him, but Emily guessed that the bad break twenty years ago that had left him with one leg slightly shorter than the other was now gifting him an arthritic hip.

Ethan had half risen to his feet, but didn't offer to help as Peter awkwardly repositioned a heavy chair to his liking, even though Emily could tell from his coiled tension that he was itching to take over.

'How did it go with Robinson—did you sort out things to your satisfaction?' he asked smoothly.

Cut off in mid-spate about her parents' past endeavours, Peter appeared momentarily confused. 'Hmm? What? Oh, yes, yes…just a trivial little personal matter,' he said dismissively as he settled into his chair.

'What? No Scrooge-like attempt to get it done on the cheap? You always used to say you hated wasting money on lawyers,' persisted Ethan with a soft chuckle that made Emily blink. 'You relied on me to deal with all your legal donkey-work.'

'Yes, well…' Peter adjusted his bow tie and smiled sheepishly. 'I know what a big shot you are these days. I don't like to trouble you with every little thing…'

'Never too busy for you, Uncle Pete.' Ethan's light words carried an undertone of seriousness that made his uncle clear his throat.

'I know that, my boy, I know…but there's no need for you to waste your valuable time on me—'

'Family is always top of my priority list. So anything you need, any time, even if it's just a rant about the latest cricket test.' Ethan grinned. 'You have my mobile number, and you know my office can always get hold of me at short notice on the radio if I'm in the air, or the satellite phone if I'm out on a remote job site.'

'Yes, of course, of course I do!' Peter's eyes darted to Emily and she responded instinctively to his slightly hunted look. She knew how uncomfortable it felt to be on the receiving end of all that concentrated attention, and she was getting the subliminal message Ethan was sending loud and clear: Peter might live alone, but he wasn't unprotected.

'Your nephew obviously has a very pronounced sense of responsibility,' she ventured.

'Yes, he does, doesn't he?' Peter enjoined hopefully, his light brown eyes latching on to the fugitive gleam that leavened her pompous statement.

'He also has a very pronounced appetite. I would have saved you another muffin if he hadn't taken the lion's share,' she continued gravely. 'That's his third.'

'Coop would have my guts for garters if I had three!' Peter perked up at her nonsense. 'You can see who the favourite is around here…'

'Tell-tale,' Ethan growled at her, his eyes smouldering with suspicion over her silent exchange of glances with Peter, even as he affected good-humoured resignation to the whimsical turn of the conversation. '*You* were eating them, as well,' he accused, sounding even more like a thwarted boy.

'Half a one,' she corrected him, pointing at the pile of crumbs on her plate, adopting a pious blue gaze.

'What about all those starving children in Africa?' He trotted out the hoary old parental reproach as being particularly apposite.

But Emily had long lived with the pressures of perceived guilt. 'It would've gone mouldy by the time it got there—anyway, I do much more good with my donations to international children's charities.'

That should have shut him up, but he crossed his arms over his chest, tipping back his head to study her with arrogant self-assurance. 'I bet you're an only child.'

It was her turn to be suspicious. 'What makes you say that?'

'Because if you had a sibling you'd know that gloating is bad form—and the quickest way to escalate a fight.'

'Then why do I get the feeling you're a champion gloater?' she shot back, and Peter laughed.

'He doesn't call it gloating. He calls it savouring victory.'

'Traitor!' said Ethan, with the twist of a smile, his eyes thoughtful as he looked from his uncle's animated expression and lively colour to Emily's spirited smile. 'But, I'm right, aren't I? You are an only child…'

Emily had to admire his dogged persistence. She shrugged. 'Yes, and even if I didn't know it beforehand I would have picked you as being a first-born.'

He threw up his hands. 'I don't think I'm going to ask.'

'I am,' said Peter.

'More socially dominating,' Emily plucked out of her memory, 'less agreeable and less open to new ideas than later-born children…'

'Ah, but you're a first-born as well,' Ethan said, finding the loophole in her theory.

'And I find you *wonderfully* agreeable,' Peter told her firmly, showing that he was well aware of his nephew's misgivings, if not the full extent of his animosity.

It struck Emily as ironic that she and Ethan were behaving as co-conspirators to keep that knowledge from upsetting him. In his presence their relationship had become one of armed neutrality.

'I'm sure you do,' said Ethan pleasantly, which was subtly different from concurring with his opinion, 'or you wouldn't be giving her such a wonderful opportunity.'

She noticed he didn't say opportunity to do *what?*

'Emily tells me that she's going to feel she's living the life of a pampered princess in the Rose bedroom,' he continued, to her sudden dismay, 'even though she'll no doubt be nose-to-the-grindstone in her brand new studio.'

Peter's lined forehead began to furrow, and Emily's fingers tightened on her water glass, the ice cubes tinkling as she hastily moistened her dry mouth, trying to think of a witty riposte that would obscure his meaning.

But it was too late.

'Emily?' Peter's puzzled frown turned to dawning pleasure. 'Does this mean what I think it does? That you've changed your mind?'

'I—um—' She hated the thought of having to back down in front of Ethan. She hadn't been thinking straight when she had flung her reckless words at his head. It had been anger talking. Now if she didn't carry out her threat she would be making herself out a liar, and he would take it as further proof of her untrustworthiness.

Trust him to put her in an embarrassing position!

'She said she was moving in today,' he was saying to Peter.

'Did I get it mixed-up, then?' Peter brushed his question aside to say happily. 'I thought you were adamant that you were quite settled in with your friend Julie…'

'Well, yes, I *was*—I am—that is, I mean—' She floundered, acutely aware of Ethan's nailing look as he realised he'd been had, and his ferocious enjoyment of her discomfort.

'You've thought about it some more and come to the decision that I was right!' Peter leapt in helpfully. 'I knew you'd come around to seeing the practical advantages! No sense in making a struggle out of things when help is there for the asking—that's what Ethan was talking about a few minutes ago, so I know he agrees with me.'

And with that whopper he reached across the table and patted her hand.

'After all you've been through lately, you deserve some pampering, my dear, and it will be my privilege to see that you get it. I realise that as soon as that damned insurance company gets its act together you'll be wanting to make other plans, but meantime feel free to treat this as your home.'

To Emily's consternation there was more than a hint of dampness about his eyes. She turned her hand over and laced her fingers through his, giving them a gentle squeeze, her heart full. She knew he had been deeply disappointed by her earlier rejection but until now she hadn't realised how much her acceptance of his generosity had meant to him. She had almost forgotten how it felt to be wanted, as opposed to merely needed. Conrad had needed her but only pretended to want her. She knew her grandfather had loved her and needed her, but his praise had been reserved for her work, and towards the end he had so not *wanted* to need her intimate caring that she sometimes wondered if he had willed himself into that last, fatal stroke.

'I-I don't know quite what to say—' She heard a muffled snort, and it provided the final impetus. Her spine straightened and she allowed her natural, warm smile to glow. 'Other than thank you, Peter. Yet again. I'm truly grateful—'

Peter's crabbed hand tightened, his grip surprisingly powerful, his reddened eyes softening. 'I'm the one who's grateful. It'll be nice to have a young woman about the place!'

'Then you should spend some of your gratitude on Ethan, too—he was the one who persuaded me that I should take up the offer,' she said truthfully.

Peter gave his stone-faced nephew a looked of startled pleasure. 'Did he really? Well, well…I owe you one, my boy.' He sat back and chuckled.

Unnerved by Ethan's silence, Emily decided it was time for a strategic withdrawal.

'Well, I'd better be off if I want to get everything done before I have to return the car,' she said brightly, jumping up.

'Shall I send Jeff to bring you over from Julie's when you've got your packing-up done there?' said Peter. 'I'd already mentioned to Coop that she might leave us something special to celebrate you moving in,' he admitted sheepishly. 'I'm a dab hand at the microwave.'

Emily chewed her lip as she thought of all the things on her rapidly growing to-do list. There was also the fact that she needed a little breathing space. She trusted Peter, but once she moved in she was going to be totally dependent on his goodwill. What if he changed *his* mind? Her stomach cramped at the thought of another round of upheaval.

'It could be quite late before I'm finished all my errands… maybe it's just better if I move in tomorrow,' she said apologetically. Preferably without the hostile observer!

'I'll be pretty shattered tonight anyway, with all the hauling I'm doing today,' she added with a wry laugh. 'I'd probably fall asleep in my soup!'

Peter looked crestfallen, but nodded understandingly and she instantly felt mean.

'I suppose it is a rather traumatic day for you,' he said, and, seeing Ethan's sharpened interest, explained about her difficulties at the house, and the lack of capacity of the borrowed old banger.

Emily had thought Ethan would have been pleased at the prospect of having more time to drip poison into his uncle's trusting ear, so she was stunned when he offered to accompany her on her next trip.

'Thanks, but I can manage,' she said shortly.

'I didn't ask if you could manage, I asked if I could help,' he said, rising to his full, intimidating height.

'But…your business suit—you're obviously dressed for work—' she murmured weakly as he unhooked his jacket from the chair.

He flicked up an arrogant eyebrow. 'I own the business. I don't have to ask permission from the boss whenever I want to take time off.' She opened her mouth; he said impatiently: 'The office knows I was planning a detour to see Peter on my way in—I didn't say for exactly how long. I've been away for several days, a few more hours isn't going to cause the company to collapse. So shall we get this show on the road…unless there's some reason you don't want my help?'

'Of course she does!' Peter chirped. 'It's just her stubborn pride talking. That car she has for a start—if it was bigger it wouldn't take her so many trips…'

'I told you, I'm not going to use the Rolls!' Emily protested.

'Right, that's settled, then—we'll use my vehicle,' Ethan told her. Her mind boggled. 'Your helicopter?'

Fifteen minutes later she was pulling boxes from the boot of Julie's dusty little car still embarrassed by her naïvety. Naturally someone like Ethan would have more than one car! It turned out that as well as the one he reserved solely for his use on Waiheke, he had another that he garaged in Peter's barn, and a company car in a permanent parking space near the downtown ferry terminal.

She found the locker that Jeff had left open for her and began transferring the sad collection of cardboard cartons, trying to ignore the sleek, silver-grey sedan slotted in next to the Rolls Royce. She wished now that she had accepted Peter's earlier offer of Jeff's help, but she knew that the reason Mrs Cooper's husband only worked part-time as a light handyman/driver was because he had a bad back, and that bending and lifting might be too much for his herniated disc.

When she looked up from her brooding thoughts her eyes widened at the sight of Ethan in jeans, a green bush-shirt and steel-capped black work-boots. From being as hard as nails, he had gone to looking as if he chewed nails for a living. In his suit he had looked cool, arrogant and sophisticated—totally out of her league. In his current garb he looked just as arrogant but devastatingly earthy and unpolished—a sexy rough diamond who wasn't afraid to get his hands dirty.

'What?' he growled, coming to a halt as she continued to stare.

'When you said you were going to change, I didn't realise you meant so completely,' she murmured, trying to conceal her dangerous fascination. 'You look—'

'What—?' he repeated, when she bit off what she was going to say.

Good enough to eat.

'Um…' She sought for something suitably unrevealing. Rumpled? No, he might think she was criticising.

'Younger.'

For some reason that made him scowl. 'I'm an engineer,' he said. 'This is what engineers wear—good for scrambling over rocks and around building foundations.'

'So why the suit?' she wondered.

'I was on my way to an appointment with some money-men, the kind who look for the gloss on their dollar.'

'Oh, but—'

'Save it. I already postponed the meet.' He picked up a box under each arm. 'Where are we putting this stuff?'

She showed him the locker. 'I hope this won't lose you their investment.'

'It won't. People who want the best are generally willing to jump through a few hoops to get it.'

'And you're the best, of course?' she mocked. 'Isn't that rather arrogant of you?'

'It's not arrogance to be certain of your own abilities,' he said, making short work of the rest of the cartons while Emily gathered the loose items from the back of the car. 'Are you the best at what *you* do?'

'I always try to do my best—'

'Not quite the same thing, though, is it?' he said. 'Although I suppose gluing old china back together is not exactly a competitive field.'

She was about to flare up at him when she realised he was being deliberately provocative. As a man who had studied the structure of materials he would be well aware of the complexities involved in any kind of restoration, large or small.

'It's a little more complicated than that,' she said, refusing to rise to his bait, although she couldn't help adding blandly: 'I actually use more sticky tape than glue.'

She gave him the keys and allowed him to back Julie's car out of the way and park it off to one side, for the sheer malicious pleasure of seeing him at the wheel of the temperamental rattle-box. She couldn't hear what he was saying but she could see the curses raining from his lips as the car did its usual bunny-hop between gears.

'Not used to a manual?' she said sympathetically as he dropped the keys back into her outstretched hand.

He grunted. 'That thing belongs on a scrap-heap!'

'Some people can't afford BMWs,' she said as they shot off down the drive in his silver bullet. 'But I'll be sure to pass your message on to Julie.'

'Where does your friend live?'

She wasn't fooled by his casual tone. 'Why do you want to know?'

'Why don't you want to tell me?'

She realised this was the start of his interrogation—the whole reason for his sudden helpfulness—and she spent the rest of the trip trying to parry a stream of similar questions with snippy counter-questions of her own, although he did manage to tease out of her a brief history of Quest Restorations by playing on her professional pride in her grandfather's unusual trade, and more about herself than she realised by displaying an insightful knowledge on the trials and tribulations of running a small business with clients who were frequently eccentric. Emily naïvely accepted his plausible explanation that his own multimillion dollar company had started off in a modest way, with a single commission to build a cliff-top house on a cyclone-prone island in the Pacific. 'The

Bunker', as he jokingly called it, had made his reputation amongst a strata of super-rich to whom degree of difficulty was more important than size.

She did realise, however, that it seemed to be taking them a surprisingly long time to get where they going—mostly because he ignored her directions whenever they conflicted with his state-of-the-art GPS mapping on the dashboard screen.

'But I know the short cuts,' she complained as they took what she felt was another unnecessary turn.

'Short cuts aren't always faster. This system factors in time-of-day traffic flows. Trust the technology.'

She rolled her eyes at his reverent tone. Trust a man.

'I work in a very low-tech, labour-intensive business. Give me hands and eyes and human judgement over soulless computers any day,' she needled.

'Computers help me create structural designs that would take endless hours of toiling with a pencil and slide-rule. They have a soul, it's just that it's incomprehensible to most—one of pure, unadulterated mathematics.'

Emily had hated maths at school. She watched his hands move on the wheel, flexing the long muscles in his forearms. The rolled sleeves had revealed that they were dusted with dark hair, which looked soft and silky against his light skin.

'You think life can be boiled down to a bunch of numbers?' she said, to take her mind off the ripple of his powerful flank as he shifted his foot smoothly from accelerator to brake. She already knew how strong his thigh muscles were, and when the movement pulled his soft jeans tight across the top of his leg she couldn't help noticing the firm bulge of the fabric cupping his crotch out of the corner of her eye. And that was when he wasn't even thinking about sex! What would he look like when he was fully aroused?

She quickly looked out her window, afraid her fevered thoughts were written all over her guilty face, the roaring in her ears drowning out his reply and making any kind of intelligent response impossible.

So preoccupied was she with trying to control her erotic imaginings that she didn't even realise they had turned into a familiar street of shabby houses until she heard Ethan's harsh exclamation and felt the lock of the seat-belt mechanism across her chest as he jammed on the brake.

'Good *God!*'

He angled into the kerb, not taking his eyes off the blackened house, festooned with bright yellow plastic warning tape across the doors and windows, which stood in the centre of a muddy and trampled garden. The right end of the lower storey was all shattered windows and skeletons of ebony wood showing through charred weatherboards, while greasy smoke and water stains smeared across the rest of the narrow façade. The wooden garage, which had been tacked onto the house next to the studio, was a pile of blackened timber beams from which her sturdy white station wagon forlornly poked its roasted nose.

'Which was your room?' asked Ethan as he got out of the car and walked around to stand on the grass verge gouged with the fire trucks' heavy tyre tracks, and boggy from overnight rain. Emily thought that he sounded shaken, but when she joined him the stern profile tilted up at the house was like carved stone.

She pointed to the dormer window above what had once been the studio, the stark pattern of black and blistered paint on the weatherboards underneath stretching up like ugly fingers to reach over the scorched window sill. In parts, the flames had licked as high as the eaves, but the corrugated steel roof, although heat-buckled in places and singed at the edges, seemed largely intact. Not so some of the plastic spouting, which had melted and sagged to stick against the side of the house like stringy cheese.

'My God, you could have died in your sleep,' he murmured, his professional eye running over the structure, identifying the likely positions of invisible load lines and support beams within the architectural skin, noting the boards nailed haphazardly up to deter intruders.

'The studio alarm woke me,' she explained. 'I inhaled a bit of smoke, that's all, when I got downstairs and tried to get to the fire extinguisher in the kitchen—'

He swung around on her. 'You didn't get out right away?' he erupted. 'What in the hell were you thinking of? Smoke inhalation is as much a killer as heat and flame...more so because it's insidious—you don't realise what trouble you're in until it's too late!'

'I know,' she said huskily, disconcerted by his anger, putting a hand to the base of her throat, remembering the raw pain of her breath sawing in and out of her oxygen-starved lungs.

'It can have lasting effects as well,' he said grimly, his steely eyes probing. 'I hope you got proper treatment—'

'I was taken to the A and E that night, and Peter insisted on sending me to his ear, nose and throat specialist a couple of days later, to make sure everything was OK.'

She waited for Ethan to ask who had paid for *that* expensive visit, but instead he just gave her a hard look and turned back to the house.

'That's everything we want there, over there by the gate,' she said, trying to turn him towards the small stack of cartons covered by black plastic rubbish bags hidden in the shrubbery. The neighbourhood was perfectly safe, but she had thought it wise not to put temptation in the way of some passing opportunist in the short time she would be away. The letter box, she noticed with weary exasperation, was already stuffed with a fresh load of junk mail.

But Ethan had other things on his mind. 'How much did you lose? I mean in terms of your inventory—how many valuable items belonging to clients were stored in the studio?' he said, walking towards the gap where part of the white picket fence had been flattened to get the fire-hoses through.

She identified the guarded curiosity in his tone and gave a sour laugh as she trailed reluctantly in his wake. He evidently thought like an insurance man.

'None, unfortunately. I've had to let our two employees go since my grandfather died so I tend to concentrate on single, high-value, complicated jobs or small bread-and-butter knick-knacks, and, since I'd just packed off a big commission from a dealer and was due to take delivery of another one from a museum the next day, I had pretty much cleared the shelves—that is, I had a couple of sentimental family heirlooms, but nothing that could be termed a treasure.'

'Why is that unfortunate? It seems to me that you were very lucky.'

'Too lucky,' she said edgily, her steps slowing as they reached the rim of the shadow thrown by the house. 'My insurance company seems to think that it's an almighty coincidence that this should happen on the one day I *didn't* have anything of great value in there…'

'The result being a lot of expensive damage but nothing utterly irreplaceable or outrageously valuable that might cause a client to make a fuss and throw up a spike on their radar,' Ethan reasoned. He nodded. 'They think you set it yourself—or had someone do it for you.'

'That's one theory,' Emily sighed, pushing at her curls, more disturbed than she wanted to let on by the abandoned air of the house and the acrid taint in the air. 'They seem to have several just as ridiculous, and all of them take time to investigate. Hey— where do you think you're going?' she cried shrilly, catching at his rolled sleeve.

He pulled the fabric free from her clutching fingers with a careless flick of his elbow, forging on towards the remains of the studio. 'Stay here. I'm going in for a look.'

Her heart began to pound.

'You can't!' She darted after him, this time grabbing his bare forearm. 'The tape's there to warn everyone to keep out,' she said, digging her heels in and feeling them slip in the churned grass, pulling her closer to the edge of panic as they neared the corner of the house. 'Until they give the all-clear only authorised people are allowed to go in—'

'I won't go right inside, I just want to look in a window or two—'

Her hand tightened. 'No, you mustn't get any closer… If you do, we'll get in trouble—'

He looked down at her white knuckles, and up again at her pale face, her lips parted by the rush of her quickened breathing, her dilated eyes jittering in their sockets.

'What's the matter, Emily?' he said slowly, the angles of his face drawing tight. He twisted out of her grip. 'What is it you don't want me to see?'

Oh, of course, his first reaction was to suspect her of something criminal! thought Emily bitterly.

'You can't see anything. It's too dark in there. It's too dangerous—' she said incoherently.

'I'll be careful.' He turned his back and took a step.

'You're trespassing!' Emily yelled, halting him in his second stride.

He rotated on his booted heel with a look of baffled outrage. *'What?'*

She swallowed, almost choking on her thickened tongue. 'This is my property and I—I'm telling you to leave right now,' she ordered clumsily. 'If you don't go when I ask, that's trespass, and I can have you arrested. I can call the police and have you arrested on the spot. Don't think I won't if you try and take another step toward that house!' Her voice rose with each progressive word in her last sentence. She must look and sound like a madwoman, she thought hysterically.

His mouth compressed, his eyes glittering slits of ice as he coldly considered the merits of her bluff. He reached into the back pocket of his jeans and pulled out a palm-sized telephone. 'Here.' He flipped it open and held it out to her. 'Take it. Make the call, if that's what you want to do, but while you're doing it I'm going to have a look around.'

He tossed it at her but she didn't even make an attempt to catch it and it spun into the grass at her feet.

'Don't,' she whispered, wrapping her goose-pimpled arms around her middle as he started to walk away again. 'What if it isn't safe? What if something falls down and hits you on the head, or you disappear into a hole and just never come back…?'

She squeezed her eyes tight shut on the endless potential for disaster. Everything that she loved, everything that she had thought was solid and substantial in her life seemed to be developing a frightening habit of dissolving like mist before her eyes, leaving her nothing but insubstantial memories.

'Nothing's going to happen to me…' Suddenly Ethan's warm hands were rubbing up and down her cold upper arms, his moist breath a clear affirmation of life as it fanned across her worried forehead, a coating of velvet on the voice that a few moments before had been cutting and dismissive of her ridiculous fears.

'Calm down, Emily, I'm not going to suddenly disappear on you, I promise.' His rock-solid bulk emanated reassuring heat, his hands settling on her rounded shoulders, kneading thumbs digging deep into the stiff muscles to release the trigger points of tension.

'I was just going to take a quick stroll around the outside of the house, well away from any overhanging bits and pieces,' he continued in the same steady tone. 'I wouldn't have broken through the safety tape. I don't take stupid risks when I'm on the job, and I'm just indulging in some professional curiosity here, OK?'

She nodded, her eyelashes still resting like thick fans against her translucent cheeks.

'Anyway, if I did get conked on the head I would have thought you'd be glad to get rid of me!' he taunted lightly.

That made her sniff, and jerk up her head. 'I *would*,' she said, her wobbly voice containing a trace of anger. 'But what would I tell Peter? He hasn't got over losing Rose, yet. He couldn't cope with losing you, too.'

Their eyes meshed, blue-on-blue, the teasing amusement fading from his face, his hands stilling on her shoulders.

'No, you're right, he talks a good fight but he's still more vulnerable than most people realise.' His fingers skimmed back down her arms and fell away, but his eyes maintained their hypnotic contact. 'How long is it since your grandfather's death—about a year?'

'Ten months,' she corrected automatically

'And you lived here in this house with him…how long?'

'Since I was seven,' she said, drawing in her lower lip.

'What about your grandmother?' he said curiously.

She looked away, breaking her trance. 'She died when I was sixteen.' Erica Quest had been a brisk, no-nonsense woman, but she had known the value of a simple hug. With her tempering influence gone from their lives, Emily and her grandfather had spent more and more time in the studio and less time socialising. Her parents' half-hearted and quite unworkable suggestion that she join them overseas and intern with one of the aid agencies had been dismissed without regret on either side. 'That was when I started my real training,' she remembered. 'There's no formal apprenticeship, you just have to learn by watching and doing…'

She took a deep breath, forcing herself to unfold her arms and affect a nonchalance she didn't feel.

'Sorry, for going off the deep end like that.' She pinned on a rueful smile. 'I don't know what came over me—'

'Don't you?' His dark, knowing tone implied a threatening awareness of her deepest insecurities. He had no right to crawl around inside her head and rummage around in her private emotions. His encouraging empathy was probably only a ruse to make her trust him. He was a prime witness for the prosecution, she warned herself. He had tried to use sex to intimidate her and now he was turning to psychology.

She ignored the seductive invitation to offload all her troubles on his manly shoulders, and shook her head. 'I don't usually throw tantrums over trifles—'

His eyes expressed his disbelief. 'You call this a trifle?' He jerked his head towards the house.

'I meant the prospect of you vanishing off the face of the earth,' she said, intent on rebuilding her crumbling emotional resistance. She put her nose in the air. 'If you want to have a look around, go ahead. Snoop all you like. The ground has been pretty thoroughly covered by experts. Fall down and break your neck for all I care!'

To her fury, instead of looking chastened at her defiant words, he merely grinned.

'You think it's going to be that easy for you to get rid of me, Emily? Think again.'

There was a sardonic satisfaction in his words, and as he strode away it struck her quite forcibly that he was doing exactly what he had always intended to do, probably from the first moment he had offered to help. All she had done with her emotional outburst was delay him for a few minutes. The outcome had never been in doubt as far as he was concerned. She had been 'handled' with superlative skill, with the result that she had ended up granting him precisely the permission she had attempted to deny!

When he reappeared around the front of the house, Emily was in discussion with a burly, bearded man, who was thrusting a sheaf of papers into her reluctant hand.

'Problem?'

For once she was pleased to feel him looming at her back. 'This is Mr Tremaine, from my insurance company—' began Emily.

'Ethan West.' Ethan reached around her to offer a powerful handshake.

The insurance man's eyes widened in recognition of the name, his manner turning from slightly supercilious to deferential.

'No problem,' he said hurriedly. 'I was just giving Miss West some forms I forgot to give her earlier—'

Emily felt the sudden tension in the body behind her an instant before he interrupted: '*Quest*. Her name is Quest, not West.'

The man looked flustered at the terse correction. 'D-did I say West?' he stuttered. 'A slip of the tongue—I meant to say, Miss *Quest* still needs to itemise some of the things for the claim—'

'That your car over there?'

Tremaine glanced over his shoulder to the nondescript blue car parked on the other side of the road.

'Yes, I—'

'You were waiting there when we arrived.'

Emily hadn't even noticed. The fact he hadn't immediately got out of his car and approached them made it very likely that he had been hanging back to see what they were up to.

He and Ethan made a fine pair of spies, she thought in disgust.

'I knew Miss Quest was coming back,' Tremaine was saying stiffly, 'and since I had another appointment in the area I decided to wait.'

Probably an appointment with one of the curtain-twitchers of the neighbourhood, Emily decided, if indeed there was an appointment at all.

Ethan moved around her and twitched the papers out of her hand, his dark head bent as he rifled the pages. 'Couldn't you have faxed these?'

Tremaine cast Emily an accusing look. 'The temporary address Miss Quest gave us didn't list a fax number.'

'Well, she's now staying somewhere that does.' Ethan shot off a number with machine-gun precision that had Tremaine's stubby fingers scrabbling for a pen from the pocket protector in his shirt. 'Once she faxes these back to you, what happens?'

Instead of humming and hawing the way he did whenever Emily had asked for details of her case, Tremaine launched into a description of the delays that had dogged the investigation, not appearing to notice he was spilling client-privileged information in the process.

'It was unfortunate that the late Mr Quest forgot to renew his existing policy,' he finished with a self-righteous pomposity that made Emily clench her fists at her sides, 'and then signed an indemnity rather than replacement policy when he took the new one out, without the proper valuation being in place—'

'Which was surely the responsibility of your company?' inserted Ethan smoothly, shuffling off the unfortunate Mr Tremaine shortly thereafter, having milked him dry of his stammering explanations.

Except for the pleasure of seeing the little man routed, Emily fumed at having been relegated to a spectator in her own affairs. She retrieved her papers and was prepared to deliver a sharp rebuff if Ethan attempted to discuss anything that Tremaine had said, but his thoughtful silence was almost worse than being peppered with questions as they got to work, fitting the remainder of her possessions into the capacious boot of his car with room to spare.

Only when they were getting back on the road did Ethan refer to the unexpected encounter.

'Does that happen to you very often?' he murmured.

Emily swivelled in her seat, spoiling for a fight. 'Does what happen?'

'People calling you West, rather than Quest.'

That took the wind out of her sails, until she realised what he was implying.

'No! And nor would Tremaine if you hadn't squeezed his hand like a tube of toothpaste and intimidated him with your bark. I don't have to trade on anybody else's name—I'm proud to be a Quest!'

She brooded all the way back to the house, this time managing to keep her comments restricted to a biting minimum.

To her relief, Ethan seemed lost in his own thoughts, content to listen to the radio, apparently no longer in any hurry to corner her with more ruthless interrogations.

She found out why when Peter greeted them on their return and insisted that Ethan have lunch with them before he resumed his flight. Back in his suit—complete with a fresh blue shirt with an unstained cuff—Ethan was the epitome of politeness over the meal, waiting until the last minute of his departure to pause and casually ask Peter if it was all right for him to stay for a few days.

'That was what I was trying to ring you about yesterday—I have a few back-to-back evening engagements coming up and it would suit me not to have to trek back to Waiheke every night,' he said smoothly, with just the right touch of uncharacteristic diffidence. 'Of course, that was before I knew you already have a—a guest...'

Peter's face turned a peculiar shade of pink and there was the faintest trace of unease in his voice as he blustered, 'Nonsense! You never even have to *ask,* you know that, Ethan—this is your second home. I'm always glad to see you or Dylan. Stay as long as you like! The more the merrier, eh, Emily?'

Oh, very merry, thought Emily, her stomach lurching as she met the bold promise in Ethan's savagely triumphant gaze.

He intended to play merry hell with her already turbulent life, and he had just awarded himself the luxury of doing it at his leisure.

CHAPTER FIVE

EMILY put down the cotton swab and adjusted the safety goggles over her eyes. Scooting her chair closer to the bench, she bent over the hard-paste porcelain vase lying cradled in the small, soft beanbag. Despite its obvious major flaws, it was still a very beautiful object.

She studied the metal rivets with which some long-dead Chinese restorer had laced together the broken shards. Dismantling, cleaning and re-bonding the blue and white vase was going to be a time-consuming task. If the rivets had been intact there would have been a case for leaving them alone, as part of the history of the piece, but these were badly rusted and the iron stains had leached into the ceramic body, and seeped along the break-lines. As well, some of the hand-crafted metal staples had worked loose from the holes that had been drilled on either side of the breaks, compromising the entire structure. A soaking in warm water had softened the plaster filling in the rivet holes, now it was going to be a matter of carefully scraping it out so that she could extract the metal without causing any more damage to the vase.

She tested the magic tape she had used to strap the unstable body together—to prevent it collapsing when she removed the rivets—and picked up her scalpel and fine dental probe. Outside it was a cloudless summer morning, and the light that streamed in through the large windows gave her perfect clarity in which to see the fine details of her work without having to use the magnifying glass that stood beside her on the bench. In contrast to the almost soundless scratch of her blade, her rescued mini sound-system rocked the studio space with the cutting-edge playlist from the university's alternative radio station.

When the first rivet came out quite easily with a cautious pull of her blunt-nosed pliers she breathed a sigh of relief that she was dealing with the right-angled variety. Acute-angled rivets would have meant she might have to resort to a hacksaw, and, although she was supremely confident now of her ability, she still remembered the carnage of her first disastrous attempts under her grandfather's tutelage, when she had wrecked many a practice piece trying to gauge the angle and pressure required to cut through thin metal without damaging the surrounding material. On the principle of learning by doing, James had got her to do some riveting herself—using the same techniques practised in the hundreds of years prior to the invention of epoxy resins—so that she would better understand the whole process. He had been more rigorous and demanding of Emily than he had of his other workers but she had respected his purpose. It was Emily who carried the family name, and must always uphold the Quest reputation for excellence.

She had done that—at the risk of her liberty and enduring peace of mind—two years ago. Although it had not been her own shoddy work that had threatened to taint the Quest name, she had been responsible for getting Conrad Nichols his job at the studio. She had been the one who had been so dazzled by his handsome face and boyish charm that she had failed to notice the growing evidence that his skills did not live up to the glowing references he had flashed at the museum seminar where they had met. By the time she had realised how cleverly he had circumvented her grandfather's stringent standards it had been almost too late to prevent a scandal.

Which made it all the more important for her to do justice to the Quest name now, she thought as she painstakingly continued to pick apart the softened reinforcing on the first row of rivets, pausing every now and then to check on some of the items she had at various stages of soaking and drying.

It was well over a week since she had settled in at Peter's and, although things were going smoothly for her within the familiar environs of the studio, life outside its walls was rocky. Ethan's 'few days' stay had stretched into four, his daily work hours erratic and only a single 'evening engagement' had interfered with his mission to harass Emily with his unsettling presence and constant, intrusive offers of 'help' and advice. The rest of his dates had apparently been cancelled at short notice, leaving him free to wedge himself firmly between Peter and Emily every night over dinner and afterwards, in the lounge, to dominate the course of the conversation until Peter's 'old bones' had taken him limping safely off to bed.

The fact that Ethan was a cynical wit and amusing raconteur only made him more dangerously fascinating to Emily's unwilling mind, and it was hard—though not impossible—to begrudge him his uncle's pride in his accomplishments. He was also a man of formidable energy and resources. He made no secret of the fact he had been making enquiries about her, it having taken him not much more than twenty-four hours to discover that Quest Restorations had been on the verge of bankruptcy for some months before and after James Quest's death.

To her great relief Ethan had eventually had to leave for the South Island, but he had returned again late yesterday evening without warning, catching her off guard as she and Peter had been huddled over his collection of old family photographs, discussing likenesses, with Emily particularly interested in the boyhood photos of the harum-scarum activities of the West brothers.

She had had absolutely no reason to feel guilty and refused to act as if she did when Ethan plunked himself down beside them on the couch, his hard thigh riffling the skirt of her light summer dress as he leaned forward to look at the album open on the coffee table.

Except…

Except sometimes the way that Peter talked, and looked at her, made her feel the slightest bit uneasy.

Not in a sexual way, never that, but just with a kind of repressed elation, a smothered air of anticipation that she found difficult to fathom. As if he was *expecting* something from her. Something that their relationship promised, but had yet to deliver.

At other times he would seem to fall into a pensive depression, becoming choked up over trivialities—something that could be as simple as her early childhood memory of learning to play knuckle bones in an Ethiopian refugee camp.

In all other ways he seemed perfectly happy with the current arrangement and, although he had at first been a trifle ambivalent about Ethan's probing curiosity about Emily, he had soon shaken off whatever doubts he had harboured and enjoyed the 'buzz', as he called it, of having other people in the house, even if they were off doing their own thing.

But every now and then, for no apparent reason, he would retreat into that fugue state, and she would look up to see him watching her with that strange, hopeful expression on his face. She was unable to shrug off the feeling that something was wrong. That perhaps Peter was suffering from more than just arthritis and an irregular heartbeat—that there was something starting to misfire in his brain. But her nebulous feelings were just that, she had no facts to support her concern should she speak out, and every reason to think Peter would be cut to the quick by any hint that she thought he was losing his mental grip.

As she teased out the last rivet and carefully turned the vase over to expose the second, more complex break, a stiff neck told her that she had been working longer than she realised, and she stripped off her goggles and pushed back her stool, rolling her shoulders to ease the muscular cramp.

She gasped when a heavy pair of hands settled on the sore spots and began a luxuriously deep, slow massage.

Tilting her head sharply back, she had a disorientating view of Ethan's upside-down face and felt the familiar, uneven thump of her heart. Whether she saw him unexpectedly, or spent time psyching herself for the encounter, she could never avoid that initial, breathless leap of delicious fright. It came from some atavistic part of her brain that recognised a hungry predator and triggered a flight-or-fight reaction. Since flight wasn't an option she had no choice but to stand her ground.

'I didn't hear you come in,' she said shakily.

'I'm not surprised,' he said, reaching over to flick off her raucous radio before returning to his task. 'You were concentrating very intently.'

Suddenly realising that the back of her head was resting against his flat belly, Emily quickly returned upright, sliding out from under his too-skilful hands. It was rather unnerving how many excuses she seemed to give him to touch her.

'Thanks, I had quite a crick in my neck,' she said, from the gleam in his eye not quite hiding her flustered awareness. 'I usually take a shake break every half-hour or so, because if you get a sudden cramp when you're doing close work…'

She was aware she was babbling as he subsided back onto the stool at the other bench, leaning his elbow on the polished top beside her open notebook and regarding her with a mocking amusement that immediately put her on the alert. He was casually dressed in fawn trousers and a classic navy polo shirt, which contrasted with the piercing lightness of his eyes. He hadn't shaved, and the dark shadow on his chin added a raw, unfinished edge to the aristocratic features. He looked lazy, but he was radiating a hidden resolve, which in her experience was a bad sign.

'How long have you been sitting there?' she asked, turning to wipe down the tools she had been using, taking the opportunity for a quick check in the shiny surface of the magnifying-glass stand. Allowing for the distortion, she was satisfied that she was presentable, her freshly washed hair spiking up in scrunched curls, her naked face unblemished by any embarrassing smudges. Now that some of her clothes had been washed and re-washed several times to rid them of their smoke-infused toxicity—she couldn't yet afford to follow the firemen's advice and get her entire wardrobe dry-cleaned—she at least had a respectable pair of jeans and a tailored short-sleeved shirt in cheerful cherry to boost her confidence.

'A while,' Ethan replied with irritating vagueness. It wasn't the first time he had invaded the studio. On his previous visit he had taken to wandering in to observe and ask questions as she had begun her preliminary examinations and was dealing with the items that only required dusting and light cleaning to be brought back to their best. Since she was on a grace-and-favour lease, she felt she could hardly order him to leave, especially as she had never quibbled at Peter dropping in for an occasional chat.

'You must have an incredible amount of patience to be able to work at such a slow pace. Don't you ever get the urge to hurry up the process?'

Emily's blue eyes widened in such instinctive horror at the idea that he lifted up his hands in surrender. 'I take it that the answer is "no".'

'If you're impatient you can do more harm than good. There *are* no short cuts to proper conservation,' she said sternly.

'I stand corrected.' He watched her subside a little at his un-accustomed meekness, the outraged colour in her eyes shading back to a more pacific blue. 'Do you usually work on Saturdays?'

'I work whenever there's work available. That's one of the big advantages of being self-employed and having a studio at hand,' she said shortly. 'I enjoy what I do, so it doesn't bother me if there are stretches when I'm in the studio seven days a week.'

'So your work is your pleasure and your pleasure is your work?' he interrupted with a soft murmur. Why did that sound indecent coming from his lips? 'It's not just that you're trying to impress everyone with your dedicated industry?'

Meaning himself, no doubt. She gave him a look of utter disparagement.

'Or that you're using work as an excuse to hide away in here,' he added silkily, aiming a far more accurate dart, 'hoping to avoid the inevitable.'

'The inevitable what?' she said, even though she knew it was asking for trouble.

The dark auburn whiskers on one side of his jaw indented with the corner of his mouth. 'Me.'

She fought down a betraying blush. 'I have a lot of lost ground to make up. Unlike you, I don't have a load of employees to take up the slack if I decide to take some time off.'

'Hmm.' It was the truth, but the deep vibration in his chest expressed his scepticism as to whether it was the *whole* truth.

'You seem to keep very detailed notes,' he said, turning his attention to her open notebook, flicking over the pages of the thick folio, filled with dense writing and drawings, in which she kept a meticulous description of every item worked on and every step of the treatment it received at her hands.

It was her Bible, and fortunately it was her habit to take it to bed to review her notes and make plans for the next day, or to research older jobs that could assist with a current work. The night of the fire she had had all three volumes in her bedroom, and several of her grandfather's, in preparation for the anticipated delivery the next day, and they were the first and only things she had grabbed as she had staggered out. The rest of James Quest's notebooks, a priceless record of a lifetime of experience, had burnt on the studio bookshelves with her other reference texts, and no amount of compensation would be able to reimburse her for that loss—even supposing the insurance company accepted that they had any real monetary value.

'I need to,' she clipped, annoyed by the suggestion she wasn't thoroughly professional. 'Would you build a house without a survey of the site or a construction plan? If there's any dispute by the owner about the way something's been done, or question about a repair, or a job has to be redone or done in gradual stages it's essential to have everything down in black and white.'

Ethan turned the pages back to the one featuring the vase she was working on, fingering the paper pocket that held the photos she had produced with the brand new digital camera and printer that she had found in one of the studio cupboards—another example of Peter's suspect over-generosity, she supposed!

'I hear my disreputable brother has turned up,' he commented idly.

She wasn't fooled by his offhanded remark.

'Yes. Coincidentally, on the very day that *you* left,' she said sarcastically. 'Complete with bags and a long story about him having to lend his apartment to some incognito movie star and his family, here to make a high-budget commercial for his advertising agency.'

He eyed the scalpel she was briskly polishing. 'Actually, I believe he *rented* his apartment at an exorbitant fee,' he said drily. 'Dylan is always open to the opportunity to make a fast buck.'

'You mean you had absolutely nothing to do with him suddenly deciding to come and stay with his dear old uncle?' she said, placing the scalpel back on the bench, out of the way of temptation. Actually she had found Dylan West fun. Flirtatious and good-looking, he was obviously a happy-go-lucky optimist who liked to skim through life without looking too deeply for meaning and motives. None of his teasing or interested questions provoked the kind of instant antagonism a mere raised eyebrow from his older brother could induce. He also had a very active social life, and did a lot of 'nipping out' in the evening, and it would usually be the early hours of the morning before she heard his Porsche throatily announcing itself in the driveway. So if Ethan had intended him as a chaperon he had fallen down on the job, she thought maliciously.

'I may have mentioned you in a fashion that might have given rise to a certain curiosity on his part,' said Ethan, picking his words with care. 'Dylan is impulsive that way. He always likes to think up ways to get the jump on me.'

Emily stared at him. What did *that* mean?

On second thoughts, maybe it was safer not to ask!

'At least he doesn't sneak around trying to catch me *in flagrante* with your uncle!'

'Is that what I do?' He stretched his long legs out in front of him, the edge of his hips on the stool, a pose of studied insolence.

'You know it is. I wonder you don't prowl the hallways at night listening for squeaking floorboards!' she scoffed.

'Oh, I can assure you there are no squeaks, this house is very soundly built,' he said mildly. 'Although as it happens I do suffer a little intermittent insomnia, so don't be surprised if you do blunder into me on some dark night...'

'Unlikely. Once I go to bed, I never budge!' she snapped.

'Really?' He quirked an eyebrow. 'That surprises me—I would have thought you were very active in bed. How disconcerting for your lover—'

'I don't *have* a lover,' she gritted, ignoring the tingling warmth flooding the pit of her stomach. 'Least of all in this house!'

'*Yet...*'

She gave a sharp cry of frustration. 'You never give up, do you? You just can't admit that you might be wrong. You're the most cynical and untrusting man I've ever met!'

'It's part of my charm,' he drawled, rising to his feet. 'You did know the appraiser's interim report had arrived?'

The swift change of subject was like a punch to the heart, turning the liquid warmth in her stomach to acid.

'I knew it was due,' she said, turning to the sink to pull on her rubber gloves and check the soiled plate she had been soaking in a plastic bowl of mild bleach solution. 'I was the one who asked for it to be done, after all...'

'Only after I'd told you I was going to suggest it to Uncle Peter—'

'But you didn't, did you?' she took pleasure in pointing out. She rinsed off the plate under the tap and placed it into a fresh bath of solution. 'You didn't seem to take me at my word when I said I was happy for an appraiser to do a valuation—I don't know why—so I insisted it be done to make sure that you'd have no reason to make any more unproven accusations.' She stripped off the rubber gloves and flung them back into the cupboard under the sink with unaccustomed lack of care for where they might land.

'Aren't you interested in what it has to say?'

She washed her hands under the cold tap in the empty sink. 'I'd rather wait for the final report—'

'He says there are at least six items which at first glance are of suspect provenance.'

'Really?' She concentrated on drying her hands and rearranging the towel on its hanger.

He stepped up behind her, alive with frustration. 'You don't seem very concerned,' he prodded.

She spun around, trying to ignore the disturbing proximity of his lean body. 'I'm not,' she said, keeping her voice calm. 'Rose has two hundred and thirty individual pieces—most of which she searched out and bought herself, all over the world, and not always from reputable dealers. I would be very surprised if some of them *weren't* dodgy—or at least not worth as much as she paid for them. It doesn't mean that fraud was involved.'

She saw the ice move into his eyes and despaired at getting him to understand.

'Even the best experts can be fooled and Rose was just a gifted amateur. She liked bargaining and she didn't specialise in one type of porcelain or era as most people do, she was a bit of a magpie—when she saw something she liked the look of, or that had an interesting history, she bought it. That's what made her collection fun for her—monetary value was never the point, it was all about the *emotions* associated with her find. Of course a thorough appraisal should be done for insurance purposes, or if a collection is being offered for sale, but I don't see Peter ever wanting to let go Rose's collection, do you? So identifying a few dubious pieces is not a disaster for him— unless it's the value your own future inheritance you're worrying about…?'

He brushed aside her angry slur as being beneath his notice. 'You didn't notice anything wrong yourself?'

Pride clawed her shoulders back. 'Are you accusing me of something?' she challenged.

His face hardened. 'I'm just asking.'

Was this some kind of trap?

'Then, without knowing which pieces are involved, I couldn't say,' she said with furious dignity. 'I've seen the full collection, yes, but I haven't handled or examined everything with an eye to authentication. I've just done cleaning and res-toration work on damaged or deteriorated items. But if Mickleson thinks that the provenance is shaky, you can trust that his research will bear out his initial findings. He has a nose for that kind of thing.'

'You know him personally?' he said sharply, as if it was a crime.

'Only by reputation. He's the best in the country. That's why I mentioned his name to Peter. I'm only surprised he could do it so quickly, he's usually booked up for months—' She broke off, having said too much. He would probably take that as an indi-cation that she had hoped for precisely such a delay.

'I paid him double his fee.'

She folded her arms in disgust. 'No wonder you think everyone is for sale—maybe for you, they *are*...'

'As you say, he has a reputation for being the best, and I never settle for less.' Again he switched topics to devastating effect: 'I understand there were a few odd rumours floating around about your grandfather's reputation at one time. About the time you and I first met, wasn't it...?'

She stiffened, her arms dropping to her sides, fingers curling into defensive fists. 'That has nothing to do with this—I don't want to discuss it!'

'Too bad, because we're going to have this discussion whether you like it or not. Were the rumours back then true? That James Quest's name was no longer a guarantee of a top-class job? Is that why the business nearly went under last year?'

'I'm not even going to dignify that with an answer,' she said desperately.

'Would you rather I make up the answers myself?' he said relentlessly. 'All I have to do is collect enough pieces to make the puzzle fit. Ask around, pay someone to do some more digging…who knows who, or what, might crawl out of the woodwork…?'

Conrad, she thought with an inward shudder. 'You have no right—!'

'Emily—' He reached out to touch her shoulder and she stumbled back, knocking her elbow against the edge of the bowl in the sink and setting the plate rattling against the plastic.

'Now look what you made me do!' she cried, stilling the plate, angry that she could be so clumsy in an environment in which she had trained herself never to make a careless or unconsidered movement. 'It's dangerous to get distracted by personal conflicts in the studio—'

'Then let's go outside—into the gardens, where there's no danger of breaking anything precious…other than ourselves, of course.'

When Emily opened her mouth to object he said with implacable intent: 'We have some unfinished business, you and I—going back two years. Until it's settled I have every right and reason to question your honesty. Trust goes both ways. If you want me to trust you, then, at some point, you have to trust me. And that point happens to be now. It's time to stop hiding, Emily. Withholding the truth is as good as a lie, and lies have a nasty way of coming back to hurt people.'

She hesitated, knowing he spoke the truth but still torn by old loyalties.

'The secret, whatever it is, *is* going to come out,' he promised. 'How do you want me to hear it—from you? Or from someone who might want to put a whole different slant on things?'

She thought of Conrad again. How he would love to dish the dirt, if he thought he could get away with it without implicating himself. And he would make her look like a pathetic, deluded fool…

She looked at the hand Ethan was holding out, palm up. Now he was confident he had won, she thought, trying to whip up a defensive anger, he could afford to act gracious!

'Come on, Emily,' he said, beckoning imperiously. 'If you're thinking of having another go at leading me up the garden path, why not do it in a real garden?'

Not so gracious, after all!

Knowing that she did, in the end, have little choice but to accede to his demands, she brushed past him and thrust her hands into the pockets of her jeans as she affected a cool saunter out the door. She pointedly stopped to take the key out of her pocket and turn it in the lock before following him down the side pathway to the shredded-bark paths that wound back and forth across the curving stone terraces, designed, so he told her, to resemble petals of a rose when seen from above.

'I didn't notice that, looking down at them from the verandah,' she murmured reluctantly, intrigued in spite of herself, as much by the subject as the tacit offer of respite from tortured thoughts of her looming confession. Or maybe it was just his cunning way of softening her up so she would be more forthcoming.

'I meant from directly above, from the air,' he said, dropping back to walk beside her through the crowded ranks of bush and standard roses arranged in subtle graduations of colour, heading for the stone steps that would take them down to the lawn in front of the pool.

Emily had been refusing to look at him, but now she shot him a brief sideways glance, her breath shortening as she found his eyes lowered to the open collar of her blouse. He certainly didn't look as if he was measuring her for a noose.

'Why would Rose do that? I thought she was afraid of flying.'

Ethan showed no sign of embarrassment at being caught enjoying the advantage of his height, explaining that although it was Rose who had originally created the idea of stepped rose gardens, over the years her love of collecting porcelain had transcended her passion for gardening, especially after her illness had affected her stamina. Since it had been Ethan who had done hard physical labour in the garden at her direction from the time he was a teenager, it had seemed natural for him pick up where she had left off, going from merely digging holes and pruning on command, to propagation, planning and planting, and eventually redesigning the whole look of the garden. He found it a good way to relax, he said to her flabbergasted face.

'*You* grow *flowers?*'

'Does that make me seem less of an ogre?' he said as they stepped down onto the emerald grass fronting the bottom terrace—a heart-stopping riot of red roses, from the tenderest bud to the most blowsy, overblown blooms trailing their petals in the breeze. 'More like someone you can talk to?'

She glanced uncertainly at him, all her tension rushing back, and he indicated the bench seat in an open-sided arbour of climbing roses, but she shook her head, disconcerted when he sat and looked inquiringly up at her. She hovered at the entrance to the alcove, fingering the tiny serrations in the dark green rose-leaves that mantled one of the trellised pillars.

'I never thought you were difficult to talk to—' she began.

'Stop procrastinating. I asked Michael about you—Michael Webber,' he added when she looked blank. 'I rang him a few days after the party, before he ducked into rehab. He didn't even remember you.'

'Thank God,' she said involuntarily, before she realised exactly what he had said. 'W-why were you asking?'

'My conscience, amongst other things,' he said, not bothering to specify what those other things were. 'I thought you might have been up to no good, and I was right, wasn't I? Quest Restorations was doing an insurance job for Sean Webber at that time, so I understand—he told me there was some cock-up with its return but that it all turned out all right for him in the end because he eventually donated it to a museum and got a tax rebate.'

'You spoke to Sean about me? *Recently?*' she said, aghast.

'Don't worry, the sleeping bulldog settled smugly back down,' he said drily. 'I only poked him very delicately during a general chat about an investment I'm thinking of making in Shanghai, which is his area of expertise. He likes to boast. I mentioned your name in passing, and he bit, but not viciously—so I guessed that whatever you had done was done successfully without his knowledge, and not at the expense of his pride or his wallet, but for a motive as yet unexplained…' The lilt in his voice made it a question, not a statement.

Emily swallowed, ripping at a leaf. 'I was desperate…'

'I get that bit.' He sounded impatient.

She took a deep breath. 'I don't know where to start—'

'I presume it has something to do with your grandfather. What did he have? Alzheimer's?'

When her eyes widened he growled: 'For God's sake, I may occasionally be a blind fool, but I'm not an idiot. You've been bloody protecting someone, and it obviously isn't yourself or you wouldn't be doing such a rotten job of it.'

She pushed back a curl that was tickling the top of her ear. 'Not Alzheimer's,' she sighed, 'but just as devastating as far as Grandpa was concerned. He developed a fine tremor in his right hand—an intention tremor, it's called—a neurological condition. His hand would tremble whenever he started to do something—it didn't happen when he was relaxed—and for quite a long while he managed to hide it from me, from everyone. But it's incurable and in most cases progressive and eventually it was getting to the point where it would compromise his work, so he got very depressed…' She looked down at the shredded leaf, folding it into little pieces. 'While this was going on I—I'd met someone—a man, at a seminar in Wellington, Conrad Nichols— another restorer, someone I felt—I thought…' She floundered, sensing Ethan lean forward, his elbows on his knees, his interest intensifying. 'He seemed very genuine, personable—'

'Handsome?'

She flushed at his cynicism. He clearly saw where this was leading. 'Very,' she said stiffly. 'He was looking for a job, so I introduced him to Grandpa and they liked each other—so he came to work with us—'

'And live with you?'

Her flush deepened. 'No, he—Grandpa was old-fashioned. Conrad had his own apartment—'

'You were in love with him.' he said flatly.

'I—he was so sunny and charming,' she admitted obliquely. 'He made it so easy to trust him. Too easy,' she added with painful benefit of hindsight. 'It was his idea that he could act as Grandpa's aid, as his right hand, I suppose—in a literal sense— so that he could keep on working. I was relieved, because Grandpa was so proud—he refused to even consider any super-visory role in the business. He'd started to scale back, and let our other two employees go without telling me, because he couldn't bear the thought of them seeing him dwindle, of losing their respect. He hated the idea of anyone pitying him. So while I was flat out trying to compensate for the dip in business by building my own client list I simply assumed that Grandpa was strictly supervising each and every thing that Conrad did, the way he had always done with me, but he was getting fatigued more easily and Conrad was taking responsibility for more of the work himself, only he simply wasn't up to it—his knowledge and ex-pertise was all superficial. He didn't have the patience to be a top-notch restoration artist, but he would have been OK if he simply worked to order. Instead he was touting for jobs under the Quest name, padding out bills, and claiming Grandpa had worked on jobs that he never even saw.

'It wasn't until we had several commissions returned asking for them to be redone that I realised what was going on, but by then Conrad had skipped out with the cash he'd creamed off the top of the bills—' She heard Ethan's explosive curse but hurried on, wanting to get her mortifying confession over as soon as possible. 'We had to pay refunds and do some free work to square things up but, thank God, James Quest's name still carried enough weight to stop the whispers in their tracks.'

Unfortunately, Conrad had left one other time bomb ticking behind him, which she had discovered when she had been combing through the notes he had left in the studio. It was a repair he had done just before he disappeared, in which he had used the wrong fixing agent, a contact adhesive rather than the capillary one that was James Quest's trademark for such delicate pieces. Even without seeing the repair itself she had known as soon as she had read of his technique that it was a botched job. Within a very short time that particular adhesive would start to change colour, and become obvious even to the inexperienced eye. To make things worse, he had already shipped the seventeenth-century Chinese flask back to its notoriously litigious owner, who would have grounds for accusing James Quest, whose signature was on a quote clearly stating the correct method of repair, of fraud or at the very least of criminal incompetence.

'Sean Webber,' guessed Ethan and Emily nodded.

'I knew he would go ballistic. He broke it himself, you see, showing it to some friend, so he was already looking to offload some blame. And he was furious that his insurance company wouldn't pay out the full value—they insisted on a restoration job and partial payout.

'I tried to ring and explain that there had been a mix-up, but I found out the Webbers were overseas. Conrad had shipped it back to them without even checking they were going to be there!' she recalled, still hot at this further evidence of his appalling lack of professionalism. 'As it happened Michael signed for it, so I thought I'd have a chance to get it back and redo the repair before Sean even got wind of it, but unfortunately Michael wasn't answering any of my messages and was always out when I called. When I did get hold of him on the phone, he wasn't interested, he told me that anything I had to say could wait until his father came home. So I got myself invited to a party there and did a temporary swap.' Remembered panic pitched her words high and breathless.

'You stole it back,' Ethan said, his voice a mixture of stark incredulity and grim admiration. 'I can't believe that your grand-father let you take a risk like that…'

'He didn't know,' she said defensively. 'He was shattered by what happened, I didn't see the point of worrying him further. And then he had a bad fall, and went for tests with the neurologist that showed the tremor was getting worse—'

'So you took the worry on yourself. What if someone had noticed you'd switched flasks? You took a *hell* of a risk!' Ethan's admiration turned to anger.

'I know, but I had to do something—and it worked,' she said, glossing over the agonies she had suffered over her brief foray into a life of crime. 'It was a simple break and it was a new one, which always makes things a lot easier. All I had to do was remove the adhesive, dismantle the flask, clean it and put it back together. It only took a few days.' A few days without sleep or solid food, in a constant state of sweating anxiety every time the phone rang…

'When Sean Webber came home he found lots of messages from me trying to contact him on his answer machine, and when he did I explained that there had been a shipping mistake, and that he had got another collector's flask—one that was fully intact, patterned differently from his, and worth more—so it was blatantly not an attempt at fraudulent substitution. He was rude and obnoxious about it when I went round to make the exchange, but not suspicious, thank God, and he was pleased that the repair on his flask was undetectable except under a magnifying glass. So it all turned out all right in the end,' she announced with an airy gesture of finality.

But Ethan had no intention of letting her get away so easily. He got up, and plucked her hand away from its act of nervous destruction. 'But how did you get a substitute flask of that quality at such short notice?' he asked. 'Surely they're fairly rare.'

She looked away, licking her dry lips. She had hoped it wouldn't come to this, but she should have known he'd leave no rock unturned.

His curiosity instantly congealed into suspicion. God, he was quick.

'Emily?' His hand tightened on hers, warning her not to prevaricate.

'Yes, all right, all right…it was from Rose's collection,' she confessed miserably, staring out at the glorious view to the distant hills of the south, sure she was confirming herself in his disgust. 'I asked Peter and he let me borrow it for a few days. He knew it was to help my grandfather, but he didn't even ask why. You probably think I took advantage of him, when Rose was so ill, and I did. I know I did. So many things could have gone horribly wrong…but when I told Peter about it afterwards he forgave me—he said he understood…'

She had little faith that Ethan would take such a compassionate view, so she was stunned when after a sizzling pause he murmured: 'You really are a hardened little crook, aren't you, Emily?'

She blinked up at his face, dappled by the shade from the canopy of twisting vines so that it was hard to read his expression in the shifting patterns. She moved back, tugging him out into the bright sunlight so that she could better interpret the strange nuance she had heard in his voice. 'So you were right about me all along,' she told him bravely.

'Was I?' he said, lowering their joined hands as he stepped closer, twining his fingers with hers. 'You mean from the first moment I saw you at that party?'

'Oh, God…' Her fingers curled over his hard knuckles. 'That awful party…it was like a bad dream—'

'And I walked right into the middle of your nightmare—'

'Looking like an avenging angel—'

'Oh, believe me, I was feeling far from angelic at the time…' He gently swung her arm across his body, brushing the back of her hand across the front of his trousers, and then back again, so there was no mistaking his deliberation—or the bold evidence of his arousal. 'Any more than I am now…'

She gasped, her hand jerking, inadvertently pushing against

the firm resilience and feeling it thicken and stir, prompting a low groan from Ethan as he turned her full against him, rolling his hips across hers in explicit invitation.

'Shall we, Emily?' he whispered huskily into her upturned face, pink with shocked excitement. 'Shall we absolve each other of past sins, and replace the nightmare with a lovely, wild, wet dream…?'

'Don't tell me you haven't fantasised about it, about what would have happened if I'd taken you up on your invitation that night,' he rasped with searing insight into the heart of her forbidden desires. 'I have, and this is how it always starts…you and I—and this…'

CHAPTER SIX

ETHAN'S HANDS SLID into Emily's hair, his mouth nibbling across her sun-warmed cheek to meet her lips, stroking them apart with his tongue, each kiss deeper and slower than the last until they were both swaying to a silent rhythm, drunk with the taste of each other. The rich, sensual perfume of the roses was suddenly more intense in the air around them, heady with notes of sweet musk, the lazy hum of the foraging bees blending with the sexy hum of Emily's body to make her very bones seem to sing with pleasure.

Her arms wrapped around his lean waist as she gloried in the freedom to touch him the way she had imagined touching him in the secrecy of her lonely bed. The hands cupping her head drifted, stroking down the sides of her neck to the hollows of her throat, splaying sensuously across the soft triangle of skin bared by the open collar of her blouse, and toying suggestively with the top button.

She ached for him to go further, but the distant drone of a small plane suddenly made her aware of their exposed surroundings and she pulled back, glancing nervously up at the verandah of the house, the flat rail of which was just visible above the banked terraces, half expecting to see Mrs Cooper peering down at them in shocked disapproval.

'Someone might see us…' she murmured reluctantly, brushing his fingers from the button, disappointed when his hands obediently dropped to rest on her waist. His eyes gleamed at the sight of her sulky lower lip.

'Not if we lie down,' he said, tumbling her down onto her back on the thick, silky grass that curved around the base of the low stone wall of the terrace.

She lay startled, panting, her short curls splayed out on a carpet of fallen rose petals as he followed her down, dropping to his knees, uttering a husky growl when he saw the tantalising gap open up between her cropped blouse and the band of her jeans. Shunting backwards, he bent and buried his face against the narrow band of honey-coloured flesh between the two strips of fabric, rubbing his rough jaw against the satiny softness, his mouth opening over her neat belly button, his warm tongue darting in to stroke and suckle at the tiny hollow.

Shivers of delight prickled across Emily's abdomen and she plunged her hands into his fire-flecked dark hair, half in protest, half encouragement.

'Ethan!' Her fear of discovery mingled with a thrill of reckless abandonment as his tongue painted a delicate line from hip to hip across her lower belly, before going back to play in the sensitive little dip. 'We shouldn't...' she quavered. 'What if somebody comes?'

She heard the deep burr of his laugh, felt it whisper damply across her quivering flesh and reverberate through his well-shaped skull.

'I'm counting on it,' he said wickedly, turning his head in the cradle of her hands and nipping at the fleshy part of her thumb. He prowled up her body on all fours, caging her with his long limbs, hovering above her and watching the fresh wave of fascinating colour sweep into her unadorned face as she realised his meaning, her up-tilted eyes the same mesmerising blue as the cloudless vault of heaven above them. At first glance she wasn't much more than ordinarily pretty yet there was something innately sensual about her that had more to do with her guarded passions than the deliciously soft, rounded body she seemed slightly embarrassed to possess. He had made a mistake, judging her on superficialities. Like the porcelain she handled with such sexy delicacy and patience, she had been tempered by her experiences into a vessel that was strong and practical, but at the same time brittle and vulnerable to careless treatment. One side of her personality was clever, cautious and controlled, but the secret, inner Emily was a bold, adventurous minx who rose spiritedly to every challenge, a tactile creature whose desire to touch and be touched was her downfall.

Even now she was revealing the dichotomy in her nature that had confused his predatory suspicions, her wide eyes expressing growing feminine apprehension while her supine body vibrated with excited eagerness, her hands absently moulding the bulging biceps of his supportive arms, teasing him with images of her massaging another swollen part of his male anatomy.

Her lips parted, silently begging him to end the sizzling suspense, and he instantly obliged, sinking down to find her mouth again, shifting his lean body to one side so that his fingers had access to dance over the front of her cotton shirt, tracing the pintucked darts that shaped it to the generous contours of her body and again finding the little mother-of-pearl button.

Emily made a little murmur, nervously tangling her hand with his, but he kissed away her conscience and dripped honeyed enticement over her brief flare of shyness.

'You're not going to make me wait any longer, are you? I wanted to do it on the first night I saw you…when you danced against me with your hands over your head, your gorgeous breasts spilling out all over me…inviting me to play. But I couldn't—I was a man on a mission…'

He was on a mission now, too, his clever fingers dipping into the vee of the fitted shirt and slipping the first few buttons free so that it split apart like the skin of a ripe red fruit to reveal the seamless white bra beneath, leaving the rest of the fastened buttons straining for release across her lower torso. For a fleeting moment Emily was embarrassed that her underwear was plain and practical rather than feminine and sexy, but Ethan seemed to find it intensely erotic, his face blurring with hunger as he looked down at his hand stroking over the smooth contours of the bra, lingering to trace around the circular shadow of her nipple, faintly visible through the opaque white fabric. He uttered a ravishingly sexy purr when it puckered at his insistent touch, pushing wantonly against the stretchy fabric, and she watched in breathless anticipation as he slowly moistened his lips, as if already savouring the taste of the dainty morsel against his tongue. Her fist clenched on his shoulder, instinctively pressing him down, but instead of lowering his head and easing both their torment his hand moved on to explore her other breast, to softly toy and tease at the burgeoning peak until she couldn't bear it any longer—hungry for everything that he had to offer…everything that she had to give…

'It opens here,' she said, impatiently guiding his fingers towards the flat plastic clip that lay between her breasts, feeling giddy as his eyes registered their lascivious approval.

'Wicked woman,' he rasped, drawing up his knee to push his heavy thigh across both of hers, trapping the restless shifting of her legs.

'You make me feel wicked,' she murmured, revelling in his teasing admiration. Confession was supposed to be good for the soul, but spilling her heart out to Ethan had also liberated her mind and body. Unburdened of the need to guard her every look and word, she experienced a soaring sense of freedom, the freedom to stop fighting her feelings and embrace the powerful attraction that had threatened to test her to the limits of her love and loyalty. Now, nothing stood in the way of exploring this exhilarating new pleasure, and perhaps finding something even more precious than anything she had lost…

Emily willingly gave up her mouth to another plundering kiss, and when Ethan broke it off in slow increments she realised he had already unsnapped her bra and peeled back the cups to expose her opulent breasts to the hot caress of the sun and even hotter stroke of his sultry eyes. She struggled to unbutton the rest of the blouse, pulled breathtakingly tight over her ribs, but he caught her hand and drew it back.

'No, not yet...I like the way it makes a lovely red frame for your pale, pretty skin,' he said thickly, placing her hand against his chest so that her palm absorbed the impact of his kicking heart. It accelerated again as he reached over and scooped up a handful of rose petals off the grass, compressing them in his fist before letting them trickle down across her naked breasts.

'Deep Secret,' he quoted with a devilish smile, watching in fascination as the dark crimson petals of his favourite rose drifted down to settle with feather-light gentleness on the two luscious mounds with their ruched pink crests. He stirred the nestling petals with his fingertips, and massaged them into her skin, crushing and rolling them into her swollen flesh and bending his head to inhale her unique, womanly fragrance.

'Now you smell just like a sun-warmed rosebud on the brink of opening...' he brushed his lips lightly up the rise of her breasts '...and feel as velvety as an unfurled petal...and I bet you taste of roses, too...' His mouth closed at last over her yearning nipple, shaping it with his tongue and rolling it against the slick hardness of his palate, drawing it deeper with a lusty growl and suckling with rich enjoyment.

The blue sky whirled dizzyingly overhead in Emily's pleasure-blinded eyes, the sunlight splintering into a kaleidoscope of piercing delight as Ethan cupped her other breast and guided it to his mouth, lapping with smooth, long strokes at the neglected peak until it glistened, inviting him to bite into its succulent ripeness and suck out the sweetness with quick, strong tugs that sent pulsing electric shocks streaking into her womb.

Hot, violent sensations tumbled through her body and Emily fought for a measure of control, her hands raking down his tapering sides and up under the thin polo shirt, to splay over the rippling musculature of his back as he moved his hips insistently against her flank, the knee lying across her legs twisting to sink between her thighs, forcing them apart.

Emily let slip a thready moan, and his mouth left her exquisitely sensitised breasts to feast on her helpless gasps of excitement.

'Are you going to unfurl for me now, Little Flower?' he murmured, and any illusion she had had of gaining control over the storming sensation was destroyed as she felt his hand glide down over her still-zinging belly button and slip under the loose band of her jeans, his inquisitive fingers finding the elastic band of her cotton bikini panties and the small embroidery flower that marked the centre front.

He chuckled as he flicked it with his finger. 'A rose?' he asked huskily.

'A daisy,' she panted, in the grip of a heated distraction. 'Sorry to be so prosaic…'

Another laugh vibrated against her lips. 'Not prosaic…a sexy wildflower, natural and free.' His thumb brushed under the elastic and into the soft, silky-warm nest.

'I see you match top-and-tail…you have cute little curls down here, too.' She heard the smile in his voice as he combed his fingers through the little triangle, tugging at it with an erotic gentleness that made her give another of the small gasps that he found so arousing.

Determined to redress the vast imbalance of power, Emily swept her hands down into the small of his back, her short nails digging into the twin indentations at the base of his spine as she sought the bare skin of his taut buttocks. She felt him shudder at the scrape of her nails and twisted to nip at the side of his strong throat, using her tongue to suckle at the wound, revelling in his hoarsened breathing, and making a sound of feverish frustration when her roving hands were thwarted in their attempt to burrow under the constricted fabric cutting across the back of his hips.

'You're going to unman me if you pull that any tighter,' he ground out, shifting his body so that she could feel the solid thrust of his swollen shaft against her upper thigh.

The gentle fingers toying with her curls extended and flexed, curving over the hot, moist bud at the tip of her sheath and dipping lightly into her wet satin core.

Every nerve and sinew and cell in her body tightened with shock and Emily's body teetered on the brink of an explosion, but suddenly Ethan was tearing himself away from her with a smothered curse, to collapse on his back on the grass beside her.

'What's the matter?' she said raggedly, bewildered by his violent withdrawal, afraid from his agonised stiffness that he was having some kind of attack…or was it another kind of spasm he was having? she wondered, her furtive gaze flicking down to a tiny damp spot on the front of his trousers. But no, the thick outline of his strong arousal still tented the fabric.

Ethan had thrown his upper arm over his eyes, masking the top half of his face. 'Brothers!' he groaned.

For a moment Emily's sensual overload continued to triumph over her mental awareness, and then to her horror she heard Dylan's voice floating out from the verandah, in a conversational sing-song that suggested he had been calling for some time.

'Emily! Eth-an! Are you down in that damned thorn-garden somewhere? I don't know where else you can be…'

Emily jackknifed to her knees, scrabbling frantically for the trailing cups of her bra, tugging them over her bouncing, blushing breasts. Ethan made no attempt to aid her panicked attempts to straighten her clothing, propping himself up on an elbow, watching with savage satisfaction as her shaking hands tried and failed to do up her bra and buttons. Muttering under her breath, she forced herself to slow down as Dylan continued to pace, now almost directly overhead.

Ethan started to climb to his feet and she dragged him down with a furious hiss.

'Wait, don't do that—he'll see you!!'

'That's the idea. Or do you want him coming down here to find us?'

He grinned as she stared in dismay at the outline of their

writhing bodies mashed into the soft, thick, perfectly mown lawn and quickly began crawling around, sweeping her hands over it, trying in vain to fluff it back up to its previous uncrushed state.

And while she was frantically doing up buttons and combing rose petals out of her hair, Ethan was calmly standing to wave up towards the house.

'Looking for us?' he called.

'If Emily's with you, yes.' Dylan sounded aggrieved. 'Didn't you hear me yelling? What are you doing down there? Were you having a dip?'

Ethan raised a taunting eyebrow at Emily.

'Don't you *dare!*' she whispered.

He threw back his head. 'I was showing Emily the garden.'

'Oh, you and your roses! Well, are you coming up…or do I have to come all the way down there and back up again?'

'You make it sound like the north face of the Eiger,' said Ethan. He continued with his raised voice: 'Ready to make the ascent, Emily?'

'Wait!' she choked, grabbing his elbow and swatting at the tell-tale grass stains on his hip and flank, relieved to notice the tiny betraying patch of dampness had faded, along with his powerful erection. 'What's he going to think if he sees these?'

Ethan looked down at her, at the crushed rose-petals peeking out of the neck of her skewed blouse and stuck to the side of her neck, the pointed outline of her nipples poking against the soft cotton of her blouse, the reddened mouth, whisker-burned throat and feverishly bright eyes.

'He's going to think I've been doing a little gardening,' he said blandly.

'Oh,' Emily accepted with a charming naïvety, then frowned in sudden suspicion when he turned away with a wholly masculine smirk.

'He's used to seeing me come in from the garden scratched and grubby,' he said, crossing to the central row of stone steps that lead directly to the verandah.

It sounded perfectly logical, she had to admit. 'I didn't scratch you,' she contested, trailing in his wake, brushing belatedly at the bottom of her own jeans.

'Not where it shows,' he said, with a dangerous edge in his voice that said he wasn't as in control as he looked. 'Now, if we go running up these stairs, it'll explain why we're all hot and bothered.'

'I thought the gardening story was going to do that,' she panted, trying to keep up with his long legs.

'That's *my* cover story,' he said as they broke out of the cover of rose-covered arches to find Dylan standing on the verandah, his hands on his hips.

Slightly shorter than his brother, he had a similar physique, although his musculature had the pumped look of someone who spent more time sculpting his form in the gym than on actual physical labour. His ash-blond hair was fine and straight, artistically tousled to fall over one side of his smooth forehead. He was dressed entirely in white, setting off the golden tan that further distinguished him from his brother, at whom he was looking in veiled amusement.

'Yo, bro—what took you so long?' he jeered, dropping his hands from his hips as they walked up to join him.

'Emily stopped to smell the roses.'

Dylan's hazel eyes briefly shifted to Emily and returned for a slight double take as she ran a nervous hand through her hair and smiled a greeting, feeling a tiny sting at the corner of her mouth.

His eyes narrowed, some of his amusement fading, and he looked back at Ethan.

'Was there some reason you wanted us, or were you just feeling bored?' Ethan asked with fraternal contempt.

'Actually it wasn't *you* I wanted at all. Didn't Emily tell you while you were on your little floral tour that I was taking her out to lunch?'

Ethan's head snapped around and Emily found herself pinned by a sharply interrogating stare.

'No, she didn't.'

His tone painted her with guilt and Emily found herself floundering for the innocent explanation. As far as she was concerned it had been a passing mention rather than a firm invitation. Dylan had so far shown himself to be a font of unfulfilled ideas.

'He—I—'

'I thought she and I could have some fun together while you get ready for your hot date,' Dylan interrupted. 'Aren't you taking the gorgeous and glamorous Carly out tonight?'

It was Emily's turn to look askance, a hollow opening up in her chest as Ethan's steady gaze flickered. Gorgeous and glamorous sounded distinctly ominous.

'Carly?' Her attempt to sound casual came out painfully flat.

'Ethan's girlfriend.' Dylan was clearly aware he was throwing a spanner in the works and was enjoying it, his brown eyes mocking the stony cast to his brother's face. 'Hasn't he mentioned that he's been seeing one of Auckland's leading female bankers for months? They're off to the ballet tonight—Carly was a promising ballerina herself, until she got too tall...'

'Dylan, cut it out!' the harsh warning came a fraction too late for Emily's gathering insecurities.

Ballet? The hollow under her heart turned into a deep, dark chasm. Not the first choice of entertainment for most males, even sophisticated, rose-growing ones. Surely a man would have to be fairly serious about a woman to allow her to drag him to the ballet? The mind-picture that was forming was not reassuring: that of a glamorous, brilliant, tall, graceful, sylph-creature.

'...but that makes her the perfect fit for a big man like you, huh? Bro—'

'Shut up!'

Ethan's voice cut him off with a surly growl, but Dylan ignored the second warning and resumed building to his big finish: 'She graduated top of her class from business school and comes from an excellent family, you know—very rich and classy. Uncle Peter is on tenterhooks waiting for an announcement. He's been dying for one of us to pop the question—'

'Dylan!' This time the harsh eruption succeeded in stopping

his stream of revelations dead, probably beçause he judged he had done sufficient damage to annoy his brother without actually provoking a fight.

'What?' His innocent grin flashed maliciously white. 'Have I told a lie? Are you not off to watch the men in tights tonight with Miss Moneybags?'

Ethan's hand slid under Emily's tensed elbow. 'Emily—'

She pulled away her arm, showing him a haughty profile. 'Excuse me, I have to go and get ready for lunch.'

'For God's sake, can't you see what he's up to? You're not going with him—'

'Of course I am,' she declared with fierce dignity. 'We have a *date*.'

'Look, Carly got these tickets for the ballet ages ago…'

He realised he was digging himself in when she said sweetly: 'Of course she did. She'd want to make sure you got the best seats. After all, second-best is never good enough for you, is it?'

She bet he never took Miss Moneybags for a quick roll under the rose bushes! No, that was for Miss Cheap-and-Convenient. Miss Rich-and-Classy was holding out for an *announcement*.

'Emily—' His voice snarled in frustration as Dylan chuckled and put a hand on Emily's back, propelling her towards the house.

'Sorry, big bro, gotta run if we're going to make our reservation. You'll have to save your explanations for later.'

'Wait!' Ethan stalked around to confront Emily. 'Before you go, tell me—whatever happened to that bastard who skipped out on you and your grandfather?' he growled.

'Conrad?' Emily could barely think past her humiliation. 'I think he went back to Wellington,' she said stiffly. 'Why?'

'You don't know his whereabouts? Because if he felt he had any kind grudge against you—'

'Oh, no—you mean the fire?' She belatedly connected with his train of thought, and shook her head. 'No, Conrad wouldn't—'

'Why? Because he was so handsome and charming?' he said sarcastically.

'No, because there'd be no profit to him,' she said, equally sarcastic. 'He knew we'd keep quiet about what he'd done because if we didn't the word would get around about Grandpa. He knew he was safe, so why would he risk coming back?' She turned to walk away with Dylan.

'I'll check him out, anyway,' he said to her back.

He was as stubborn as he was perfidious.

'You don't have to—'

'I *said* I'd check him out.'

'Fine. Do what you want. You will anyway.'

She stomped away, and missed Dylan flipping his brother off before hastening to follow her.

Emily got almost all the way back to the studio before she realised Dylan was sauntering at her heels. She halted.

'Oh, look, about lunch…I really should be getting back to work. I left some things soaking that I need to check, and I really don't think I can spare the time…'

He waited for her excuses to peter out before he tilted his blond head to one side and wheedled: 'Oh, come on, you have to eat, don't you? I know this fabulous little fish place down on Eastern Beach, we can be there in twenty minutes—'

'You mean the place where you made the reservation?' she said wryly.

He looked boyishly chastened, but his hazel eyes twinkled.

'So you'd rather lunch here…sitting across the table from good old Ethan.'

She hadn't thought of that. Her stomach curdled at the idea of confronting him again so soon…and in front of Peter, who was hoping his nephew would soon be engaged. She was a gullible idiot to have assumed that just because she had cleared the air over the past, she and Ethan were free to act on their attraction. Her fantasy of a relationship with him was a creation of her own emotional needs. The sad reality was that to Ethan she was just a physical itch to be scratched.

'Or I could just have a sandwich while I work,' she

murmured, recalling how Dylan had played his own part in her painful disillusionment.

'But think of all the fascinating conversation you'd miss,' he said cunningly, plucking a mangled rose petal and a blade of grass off the back of her blouse and pressing them into her palm. 'You could tell me all about you—and I could tell you all about Ethan…'

She didn't remember the rest of his argument, which was extremely persuasive, but an hour later, after a short delay to refresh her soaking solutions and note down the times, Emily was hungrily forking up seared scallops and sipping cautiously at an excellent Sauvignon Blanc while she listened to Dylan talk about the change that had come over his brother after their parents' deaths. Prior to that, he said, Ethan had always been up for a bit of fun, but, although he had risk-taking in his blood, he hadn't possessed the impetuosity or sheer flamboyance that had characterised their father.

'Ethan blames himself for the way Mum and Dad died,' said Dylan, his mobile face more sombre than Emily had ever seen it, 'because he was supposed to be with them that day. The three of them were flying down to a wedding in the South Island, and Ethan was going to pilot the plane because he was trying to build up his flight hours. But some problem came up at work that delayed him. He thought it wouldn't take him too long, so they kept bumping the take-off time, but in the end he had to flag the trip altogether. By then it was quite late in the afternoon and the weather had started to pack up, but Dad being Dad wasn't going to let a little low cloud stand in his way. He could have waited until the next morning, but he didn't want to miss the stag party, and Mum was typically more worried about getting down there in time to have her hair done than a bit of bumpy weather—especially with her darling "Ace" at the stick.'

Dylan topped up his glass and toasted ironic fate. 'Dad also knew that he was going to be bankrupt again in a few days. The receiver was poised to pounce on his assets, including his personal plane, and Dad wanted to get a last flight in—as it turned out it was *literally* his last flight,' he finished with a sardonic wryness that made him sound for the first time like his brother. 'They went down in rugged bush country—it took days to find the wreckage, but they'd both been killed instantly. Dad flew right into the side of a hill.'

'Oh, my God, how terrible,' said Emily, clutching her glass, imagining Ethan's feelings on hearing the news that his parents' plane was missing. She knew instinctively that he would have flown with the air search.

'But your father—he ran an airline, surely he was an excellent pilot—'

'Oh, sure, but even good pilots sometimes make bad decisions.' He shrugged. '"Pilot error" the report said—for some reason Dad was trying to fly under the weather rather than using his instruments and must have got disorientated. Of course, Ethan is convinced that if he'd been up there with them it wouldn't have happened, but he wasn't instrument-rated himself at the time, so who knows? Ethan would never have even taken off with the cloud as low as it was, but Dad was a real gung-ho competitor and would have done it anyway just to prove that he could. Dad used to josh him about it, but Ethan has always been a cautious flyer, mainly because he doesn't really enjoy it. I think he only took it up because Dad was disappointed not to have a son who wanted to follow in his footsteps.'

'You don't fly yourself?' asked Emily, slightly surprised, for he certainly had the dashing air of someone who liked to seek new experiences.

'Are you kidding?' His grin was charmingly self-deprecating. 'Always looked too much like hard work to me. Give me a fast car any day—just jump in, pick up your girl, and you're off!'

She laughed, not wholly accepting his estimation of himself as a total lightweight, he displayed too much insight to be as shallow as he pretended. Which he proceeded to prove as he said:

'After the crash Ethan gave up flying for a while—got a real bad case of the heebie-jeebies—but then he forced himself to go back to it... I think he saw it as a kind of penance.'

'But surely he can't really believe himself responsible for the crash—or decisions he had no part of—?'

'*Intellectually* he knows he's not to blame, but emotionally it's an entirely different matter. I don't know whether he's more angry at Dad or himself for what happened that day.' He sighed. 'All I know is, since then he's tended to have a vastly over-developed sense of responsibility towards the rest of the family.'

'You mean you and Peter.' She realised now why Ethan had come down on her like a ton of bricks when he had suspected her of conning his uncle.

'He can be a pain in the neck sometimes—always seems to know what I'm up to, as if I'm sixteen rather than twenty-six.' Dylan pulled a long face.

'And, of course, you give him no reason to ever worry about you,' she said drily.

He looked pious. 'I consider it my duty as a brother to give his paranoia a thorough workout every now and then.'

'Like teasing him about Carly?' said Emily, who had been waiting to casually slip the name into the conversation.

'Who?'

Dylan grinned as she tried to hide her frustration at his puzzled reply.

'Oh, *her*…Carly Foster,' he said, leaning forward, his elbows on the table, his voice sinking to a mock-confidential level. 'A real fox. She and Ethan have been dating on and off for a few months now.'

'On and off?' Emily chewed a scallop without tasting it as she considered the phrase. It didn't sound as committed as he had made it sound back at the house.

'Well, they're both busy people—but Carly's pushing thirty, her biological clock is ticking, and most eligible bachelors in her price range tend to marry sexy young things who massage their egos rather than women who compete with them. She's been trying to corral Ethan into realising what a perfect couple they'd make, but he's proving far too elusive for her….'

Emily put down her fork, furtive hope creeping back to ease her humiliation. 'You mean…you don't think—? They're not—?'

'Having an affair?' Dylan shrugged. 'They're adults, both attractive, why wouldn't they go to bed together?' His narrow face took on a moody look and his voice hardened as he answered his own question: 'But, no, I don't think Carly would take the risk of giving it away for free. She's using a time-honoured ploy—keep him dangling until he's so desperate for it, he'll offer her the brass ring—or in her case it'd have to be platinum. She doesn't seem to realise that Ethan is the king of self-denial,' he said with a hint of relish. 'After the Anna thing he learned to be very wary of women with personal agendas—'

'The Anna thing?' Emily grabbed her wine and took a fortifying sip. Did she really want to know?

Who was she kidding? Of course she did! 'Who's Anna?'

'Old news,' said Dylan. 'Ethan was engaged when Mum and Dad died. But Anna dumped him when he poured all his money into debt repayments instead of the big wedding and new house they'd planned on buying. He took on a load of unnecessary pain after the crash, working to pay off all Dad's creditors, especially the employees and Mom and Pop investors, even though legally there was nothing left in the estate. He accepted a little bit of help from Peter, but mostly insisted on taking care of it all himself. Wanted me to be able to be proud of our family name. See what I mean by over-responsibility?'

What Emily saw was a similarity between what she had done for her grandfather, and Ethan's self-sacrificing effort to make good his father's losses. When he had listened to her explanation, he would have understood exactly what she had been going through. And, like Conrad, his fiancée had also proved to have feet of clay, melting away when the going got tough. He must have been devastated. Perhaps that was why he now preferred his ongoing relationships to be on a less emotional footing. Dylan obviously didn't like Carly as a wife for his brother, but Ethan himself might be actively seeking a practical arrangement rather than a love match. Family was important to him. Perhaps it was *his* biological clock that was ticking!

A few glasses of wine were not an ideal preparation for an intensive afternoon's work so when they got back to the house Emily slipped away to her room with a black coffee and did some reading. She was *not* hiding, she told herself as she quietly clicked the lock on the door and lay down on the cool coverlet with her notebooks. Protecting oneself from hurt wasn't hiding, she repeated to herself a little while later when there was a series of soft knocks at the door, and Ethan's voice called to her through the wood. She watched the handle turn, and fed on the grim frustration she could hear in his voice when he concluded she was in her room, but deliberately ignoring him. She listened to him retreat down the hall, fighting the desire to rip open the door and call him back. She knew what would happen if she let him in…he would touch her and she would be lost to herself again, sucked into the sexual maelstrom where nothing mattered but the next rapturous thrill. There was no shame in admitting his power over her, the shame would be in letting him use it at the expense of her self-respect.

Strangely, she had never been jealous of Conrad, although he had flirted with practically every woman he met, but the idea of Ethan with another woman made her feel sick, and she couldn't trust herself to discuss the matter rationally. She was afraid what she might betray. She didn't want to hear that she was just a passing phase in his life, a piece of 'unfinished business' that he wanted to finish off so that he could move on to better things.

Neither, knowing what she now did of his background, did she want his pity, compassion or understanding.

What she wanted from him was something that she wasn't prepared to acknowledge, even to herself. She had enough of an emotional struggle on her hands just to survive from day to day, she couldn't afford to take on another, unwinnable, battle.

So when, just before dinner, she unexpectedly encountered him on his way to the front door, dressed in the black-tie splendour that gave her a shock of *déjà vu*, she froze like a doe in a hunter's sights.

'I thought you'd already gone,' she muttered. Apparently the ballet was more than just dance—there was a fundraising champagne dinner beforehand and an after-party backstage.

'So you thought it was safe to come out?' He shot his cuff and glanced down at his watch, a muscle clenching in his cheek as he looked back at her with banked anger in the steel-blue eyes. 'You can't avoid me forever, Emily.'

'I don't ask for forever,' she said tightly. 'One day at a time will do.'

His eyes narrowed. 'None of us get forever. Which is why we have to make every day count.' He uttered a smothered curse at her frozen expression and swung on his heel.

'*Tomorrow,*' he ground out, a threat and a vow, delivered over his elegantly clad shoulder as he strode away to meet the gorgeous and glamorous Other Woman in his life.

Or perhaps, the thought occurred chillingly in the wake of his words, he intended to make *Emily* the Other Woman.

CHAPTER SEVEN

'OH, WOW, this looks exactly like me when I was this age!' Emily exclaimed in laughing surprise as she studied the faded colour photo of a shapely, curly-haired teenager in jeans and a tee shirt, standing awkwardly beside a flowering bush, her arms folded defensively under her plump breasts, a half-smile pinned to her lips. The shape of her face and eyes, and even the tilt of her head, was so similar to her own it was like looking in a mirror.

She glanced at the back of the photograph, but there was nothing to identify it, unlike most of the other old prints, which were labelled with Rose's distinctive flowing script stating date, place and the names of the people frozen in their timeless poses.

Peter looked at it, but didn't take it from her, his hands restlessly squaring up the rest of the photos spread out on the dining table. Emily's encounter with Ethan had taken away her appetite, but she had forced herself to eat a proper dinner to refuel her ebbing supply of energy, and had readily agreed to join Peter in another of his meandering strolls down memory lane when a rather abstracted Dylan had wandered off, presumably to brood on his somewhat astounding lack of a date on a Saturday night—or more likely to plunder his little black book for last-minute opportunities.

Emily was eager for anything to divert her from her own desire to brood. There was no sense in tying herself in knots over what might or might not happen *tomorrow*. She could have watched television, or a DVD from the extensive collection in the games room, but that would be rude when Peter obviously preferred human conversation to the electronic entertainment that kept him company when he was on his own.

'This is amazing,' said Emily, inspecting the girl's face again, wishing the eye-colour hadn't faded too badly to determinate. 'Who is it—do you know?' she asked.

Peter cleared his throat, fingering the handle of his coffee-cup, but deciding not to drink. 'My daughter.'

'Your *daughter?* But I thought—' Emily stopped, realising too late what it meant, and stricken by the pain she saw in his face.

'That Rose and I couldn't have children? We couldn't, not together. Rose had a hysterectomy in her early twenties,' he said stiffly.

Emily struggled to hide her shock. 'I'm sorry, I'm sure it's none of my—'

'We went through a pretty bad patch at one stage—' he laboured on, to her intense embarrassment, his eyes fixed firmly on her flushed face. 'Rose was obsessed about not being able to give me children, and tossed me out of the house. I was bitter, and—I won't fancy it up—I had a fling with my secretary. It only lasted a few days, because when Rose changed her mind and asked me back I was there like a shot. I offered Maria a job in another part of the company but she resigned on the spot.' He hunched his thin shoulders in a regretful shrug. 'I'm ashamed to say I was glad she was gone… I didn't want her around reminding me of what I'd done, and I was afraid if Rose found out she'd toss me out for good. Rose was the only woman I ever loved, I ever wanted…'

'Everyone knows that,' said Emily, shifting her chair closer and patting his hand uncertainly. 'You and Rose were married for, how long—?'

Peter's chin lifted. 'It would have been fifty years, if she hadn't gone and died on me. And I never strayed before or since—only that one time.'

'But—there was a child?' Emily's mind reeled from the appalling ramifications as she looked down at the photograph lying on the table. Was Peter about to confess he had been supporting a secret second family? She didn't think she could bear it. 'Are you sure the baby was yours?' she ventured delicately.

If anything, he looked even more ashamed. 'It was Maria's first time. She was nearly forty—ten years older than me; it never occurred to me that she might get pregnant…'

Emily locked her jaw to stop it dropping, although she supposed it was better than the idea of Peter preying on a vulnerable young employee.

'Anyway,' said Peter, 'I didn't know anything about a baby. Maria never told me she was pregnant. She just quit and disappeared. Then, twenty years later, I got a letter from her, posted after her death. She told me about Carol—my daughter—her wild-child, she called her, and sent that photo. Said she was sorry, but she hadn't wanted to wreck my marriage, or risk any chance of me trying to take the baby for Rose.'

'So, what's she like?' asked Emily warily. 'Your grown-up, wild-child daughter?'

'I don't know,' he said, sounding very old and bitter. 'That's the only photo I have. She didn't get the chance to really grow up. She was dead herself at nineteen. Got mixed up with some drug-running crowd and died in rather murky circumstances in Indonesia while she was living there with her boyfriend.'

'Oh, God…Peter! So you never even got to meet her?' Emily realised in horror. 'This is all you have left of her—a photograph and a letter?' No wonder he was bitter.

'I know a lot more than I did. I had my lawyers investigate, but I couldn't act on any of the information while Rose was alive—that would have been like my being unfaithful all over again. I couldn't let her know how badly I'd let her down. And knowing that there'd been a baby…well, that would have tormented Rose even more than it does me.' Peter's thin voice faltered, then strengthened. 'But now she's dead I can at least try to make some amends. You see, Carol was pregnant when she went to Indonesia. She died not long after she had the baby…'

The light dawned as she recognised the emotion he was trying to suppress. 'You have a grandchild!'

Peter nodded, his voice thickening. 'A granddaughter. One who makes me very proud.'

Emily's own throat tightened. 'That's wonderful. I'm glad for you. So something good has come out of all the turmoil.'

'Of course, no one knows yet, except you—and the lawyers, of course,' he continued shakily. 'I—I wouldn't know how to tell the boys. They thought the world of their aunt Rose.'

'Of course, I understand,' she murmured, not quite certain he was right, although she could well understand his reluctance. She suspected that Ethan would resent being deliberately kept in the dark as much, if not more, than he would be angered or shocked by the revelation of a forty-five-year-old indiscretion. 'So your granddaughter—she lives in Indonesia?'

Peter gave her a strained look. 'Oh, no, she was adopted by a New Zealand couple.'

Seeming to suddenly need something to relieve his tension, he picked up a piece of the crunchy, low-calorie chocolate slice Emily had made to have with their coffee and began nibbling at it as he told her the story his investigators had put together.

There had been a huge cyclone and terrible floods, and the whole region had been in chaos when Carol had given birth. She had been hiding at a refugee camp under another name, having fled her drug-dealing friends, afraid of what they'd been planning to do to her baby. She'd had infected wounds from a beating and had begged for help from the two idealistic young Kiwi aid workers who had been with her for the difficult birth, a man and wife who, when they had later found her delirious and dying, had ended up smuggling her daughter out of the country as their own. Carol had only ever told them her first name, and that she had no family, perhaps in the hope that would more incline them to keep whatever promises they had made to the dying girl.

Emily listened to the tale with a puzzled air, until he mentioned the date of his granddaughter's birth. She drank from her rapidly cooling coffee, trying to ignore the strange ringing in her ears. She had a horrible feeling that Peter's strange looks were now explained, and that his benevolence had not been a simple case of friendly concern. 'What a coincidence—that's when I was born,' she said, trying to sound upbeat. 'And my parents were in Indonesia on flood relief work, too…'

'It wasn't a coincidence, Emily.' Peter had obviously decided it was time to stop beating about the bush. 'Your parents were the ones who adopted Carol's baby. *You're* my granddaughter.'

'But I can't be!' she said firmly, looking at him with deep compassion for his mistake. Oh, God—Ethan had been right all along to insist that there was a lot more to Peter's kindness than met the eye. 'I'm sorry, but you're mistaken. It's not me. It can't be—I'm not adopted.'

'Are you sure?' he said, taking another bite of his comfort food, using the grinding motion of his jaw to conceal his trembling mouth. 'Because I have reports—' He gave a little cough. 'Oh, dear—I just assumed your parents would have told you—'

'Of course I'm sure,' she cut in. 'I've seen my birth certificate. And you're right, they *would* have told me.'

And if Peter had been her grandfather, that would mean that James Quest hadn't been—and yet he had constantly talked of the continuation of his skilled trade through the family line, of his satisfaction at being able to pass on his heritage to his son's child. She didn't believe he would have put the same emphasis on their relationship if she had been adopted.

'Unless they felt they had a compelling reason not to—'

Like a promise to a dying woman?

He was growing increasingly agitated, but she couldn't let him go on believing something that wasn't true just because she didn't want to upset him.

An hour later her emotions were still in a gigantic knot as Ethan burst through the lounge doors and strode over to his uncle, lying propped up by cushions on the couch, a light mohair blanket over his lap.

'What in hell happened? Are you all right?' He glared at the doctor. 'Was it a heart attack, Mike? Why isn't he in hospital?'

Emily stared at him as he wrenched impatiently at his black tie, stripping it off and shedding his close-fitting jacket onto a side chair as the doctor placed his blood-pressure monitor back into his large bag, and soothingly explained that there was no need for hospitalisation, that it had been a simple case of choking, and Mr Nash's lungs were now perfectly clear.

'If it was so simple, what are you doing here?' Ethan demanded sharply. 'And why am I missing the last Act?'

Emily whirled and looked accusingly at Dylan, who expressed helplessness with his hands. 'You called the doctor,' he murmured. 'I had to do something, so I sent a text to Ethan. He would have eaten me alive if I hadn't let him know something was up.'

Ethan's head had swung round as he heard Dylan's voice. '"Uncle had turn. Doctor on way,"' he quoted angrily. 'Do you think I was going to sit there and enjoy the rest of the ballet after reading that?'

'You left your phone switched on at the ballet?' commented the doctor with the ease of familiarity. 'You're a brave man, that's all I can say.'

Ethan speared him with a look. 'I had it on vibrate. I tried to call, but I kept getting an engaged signal and you weren't answering your cell,' he accused Dylan.

'I must have left it in the other room, and maybe the land-line receiver wasn't put back properly after the phone call to Mike. There *was* a bit of a panic on,' Dylan defended himself, and Emily too. 'You know what Uncle Peter's like, he was insisting he was OK, but Emily was concerned that there might be something else wrong—he did look rather grey and his chest was pretty wheezy. Emily had to perform the Heimlich manoeuvre, she says, and she was worried she might have broken a rib…'

'So you weren't here when it happened?' Ethan's gaze switched to Emily, who was sure she looked a picture of guilt. Ethan had driven all the way back from town in his current state

of anxiety? He could have had an accident, she thought wretchedly. Why had Dylan done it? He had been the one telling Emily
she was overreacting!

'I was in my room, making a few calls—' Dylan said, as Peter
interrupted croakily.

'For goodness' sake, Ethan, calm down and let poor Mike get
back to his family.'

'Yeah, thanks, Doc, don't forget to send us the bill,' grinned
Dylan, and the doctor eased himself past Ethan, patting him on
his stiff shoulder.

'He's perfectly fine for his age and condition, Ethan, but it was
good for me to come and check him out, just to make sure. Honey
and lemon will help his sore throat, and he should try not to talk
too much for a day or two. He just gave himself a bit of a fright.'

'He apparently gave us all one,' said Ethan.

'Yes, well…it's you who'll be in danger of a heart attack if
you don't learn to control that type-A personality of yours.
Maybe you should take up yoga.'

'Are you going to bill us for that little piece of medical insight,
too?' said Ethan, sending him sarcastically on his way before
looking back down at his uncle.

'Exactly what did he choke on?' When Peter opened his
mouth he held up a warning finger. 'No, not you, you're not
supposed to talk. I was asking Emily.'

Peter subsided gratefully, and Emily moved over by the couch
to admit: 'It was a bit of chocolate slice.'

She was trying to act normal but she was acutely aware of the
need to step around the invisible elephant in the room, the subject
that she and Peter had barely begun discussing when he had
suddenly started choking.

'*Chocolate?*' The word was redolent with criticism.

'He's allowed treats. It was low-fat and I used sugar substitute, and it had almonds for his heart,' Emily said, pressing her
lips together as she became conscious that she was gushing.

A flash of sequins caught her eye and she noticed for the first time the woman who had followed Ethan into the room. Or perhaps glided would be more apt because she seemed to float rather than walk. To Emily's chagrin, she was even more beautiful than her advance publicity had implied. Tall and ultra-thin, her blonde hair caught up into a smooth chignon, she wore a full-length dress of dark green silk organza, with sweeping skirts, the see-through bodice strategically beaded and lace-embroidered because there was obviously no need for a supportive bra.

Emily immediately felt like beggar-maid in her print shirt-dress and espadrilles. Her nose was probably shiny, too, and her hair still standing on end.

Ethan noticed that she was trying not to stare and made a barely civil introduction, obviously impatient to get back to the matter in hand.

'Carly Foster, this is Emily Quest—you may remember I told you about her…'

They had talked about her? Emily's skin crawled as she suffered the fleeting touch of an ethereal hand and managed a brief smile in answer to a polite greeting. In the interests of fairness, Carly should have had a voice like Donald Duck, but fate proved unkind and her tone was as flawlessly smooth as her beautifully tanned skin, her dark brown eyes disturbingly resentful.

'And, of course, Dylan you know,' Ethan added in a voice so dry it crackled, waving at his brother, lounging against one of the room's decorative pillars.

'All too well,' murmured Carly sweetly, but Emily supposed it was a measure of Dylan's dislike that for once he didn't bother with a teasing comeback, merely shrugging in a silent 'whatever'.

'So you were just sitting here eating quietly and he suddenly choked.' Ethan had returned like a dog to his meaty bone. 'That doesn't sound like Uncle Peter. He doesn't bolt his food; he's usually a very fastidious eater.'

'Not here, we were at the table in the dining room, talking and looking at photos—'

'Photos of what?'

'You on a bearskin rug, probably,' chimed in Dylan. 'You know, the ones showing those cute dimples on your—'

'Dylan, shut up,' growled Ethan for the second time that day.

'Of people. Family. You know, just old photos…' Emily trailed off, looking at Peter out of the corner of her eye, but he was lying limply back against the cushions, making the most of his indisposition. They had left the photographs on the table when she had leapt up to Peter, suddenly realising what his watering eyes and soundless gagging meant. Would Ethan notice that one, anonymous photo amongst many or see the resemblance that Emily had yet to convince Peter was only coincidental?

If Emily had been the ethereal type she could have put a hand to her forehead and feigned a swoon, but she was regrettably solid and didn't think Ethan would buy it for a moment.

'And what did you say you were talking about?' He followed her sneaking glance and frowned. 'Was he upset about something? Were you having some kind of an argument that set him off?'

Emily felt the invisible elephant's hot breath on the back of her neck. 'We weren't *arguing*…' But her equivocation cost her dearly, for he squared off in front of her, his shoulders blocking out everything but himself and the focused intensity of his gaze.

'But you were having a disagreement about something, weren't you?' he rapped out. 'What was it?'

Faced with a direct question, Emily quailed, unable to bring herself to utter an outright lie. She had thought she was done with damaging secrets. If she started lying to him now, she would lose all the ground she had gained with him this morning, and more… She would be tangling herself ever deeper in a family problem where she had no right to be.

Her hesitation stretched for an eternity, although it was probably only a few seconds. Suddenly she felt Peter's icy fingers groping for her hand and squeezing it lightly, and shifted to see the open plea in his brown eyes. He was begging her not to expose his shameful secret to his family before he was ready to do so, not to humiliate him in front of Ethan and his lovely, sharp-eyed guest. He had only told Emily his story in the belief that she was his granddaughter. She had no right to betray knowledge gained through a false confidence.

'I'm afraid I can't tell you,' she said quietly, squeezing Peter's cold hand back in silent reassurance before tucking it under the folds of the lap blanket. 'It's something private, between Peter and I.'

Ethan had watched the brief clasp of hands with baffled annoyance; now he wrapped his fingers around Emily's elbow.

'Will you all please excuse us for a few minutes?' he demanded pleasantly, whisking her out of the room and across the hall into the games room, where he backed her up against the side of the billiard table.

'All right—what's really going on?'

She looked at him in disbelief, her hands gripping the polished edge of the table behind her. 'I just told you—I can't talk about it.'

His dark brows drew down over his eyes, his granite jaw jutting as he moved closer, almost blinding her with the dazzling white of his broad shirt-front. 'He can't hear you from here,' he said in a lowered voice, tacitly inviting her to lean on his strong shoulder. 'Whatever you tell me, I won't let it get back to him—'

'That's got nothing to do with it,' she said staunchly, seeing his tactic for what it was, an attempt to suborn her allegiance. She still couldn't get her head around the disturbing set of coincidences and longed for an unbiased view, but she wouldn't get that from Ethan. 'It's no good badgering me, I'm not going to tell you.' Let Peter have that painful duty himself.

She made the mistake of looking straight up into the icy blue eyes and her foolish heart softened at the storming conflict she saw there. How could she condemn him for loving his uncle and caring deeply for his health and welfare? She knew all too well what it was like to be held at arm's length by an old man's pride. 'He's not gravely ill or dying, Ethan, if that's what you're worried about. He just has some…' she hesitated '…some issues—about the past.' She straightened her shoulders. 'And that's as much as you'll get from me. If you have any more questions, you'll have to address them to your uncle. But if I were you I'd let him do it in his own time.'

'Oh, I see—you're the family expert now, are you?'

She flinched and turned her head away, but he brought it back, his hand firm on her chin, tilting it so she couldn't avoid his arrested look.

'What? What did I say?'

'Nothing.' The chill that had invaded her when she'd thought Peter was having a heart attack had been replaced by a pervasive heat. Her heart quickened. She was supposed to be resisting him with every fibre of her being, she reminded herself, not aching to turn her cheek against his controlling hand.

He shook his head, chiding her for the blushing untruth. 'Oh, Emily, you're so—'

'So what?' she said, bracing for another attack.

'Damned stubborn,' he said, but it wasn't an insult. His hand fell away but he still stood disturbingly close. 'And loyal. To a fault. First your grandfather, now Uncle Peter.' If only he knew the irony of his words. 'When do I get my turn?'

His sudden gentleness was even more dangerous to her defences than his sharp perception. Her fingers dug into the wood behind her back. As he said, trust worked two ways.

'Hadn't we better be getting back to the others? Carly must be getting impatient—'

'Carly can look after herself,' he said, not budging.

'That's not very gallant,' she said, trying to sound reproachful.

'She's not dating me for my gallantry.'

The sweet thrill in her veins soured. 'How passive that sounds. I thought you were dating *each other*.'

'We have a long-standing arrangement—'

'Oh, so now it's not a date, it's an *arrangement*,' she cut him off in a voice that dripped sarcasm, her blue eyes huge with disdain. 'I suppose we could stand here arguing semantics all night, but I wouldn't want you to miss your backstage party.'

'It's not *my* party. Carly's a patron of the company—'

'How wonderful for her.' She tried to dodge past him but he placed his hands on the table on either side of her hips.

'Emily, you don't have to worry about Carly—'

'It's not tomorrow yet,' she gritted at him, standing rigidly within the frame of his arms, her senses flaring at the proximity of his heated body. How could he dismiss the other woman so lightly when she was right there across the hall? 'I still have a few hours of avoidance to go, and if you don't mind I'd like to be free to enjoy them.'

He vibrated with a frustrated tension that gave her a furious charge, and she half expected him to kiss the scornful words off her lips and show her exactly what he knew she'd enjoy.

Instead he mastered his unruly impulses with an impressive display of self-control.

'What do you really want from me, Emily?' He asked the unanswerable question, and turned away without waiting for her response.

An angry little bomb exploded in her heart.

'And, by the way, Emily,' she said, putting on a deep, sarcastic voice: 'I forgot to say this in my rush to find you guilty of neglect, but thank you for saving my uncle's life tonight.'

He turned back with startling swiftness, yanked her close, and planted a short, hard kiss on her complaining mouth.

'Thank you. You're a heroine.' His genuine gratitude took the furious wind out of her sails. 'I wish I'd been here to see you in action.'

She wished it, too. If he'd been with them, she would still be living in comfortable ignorance.

She took a steadying breath. 'What? And missed the men in tights?'

'You're spending too much time with Dylan. You're even beginning to sound like him,' he murmured, hustling her back to the lounge. 'But I might have a remedy for that.'

When they walked into the room, Peter was looking apprehensively towards the door, while Dylan and Carly were off to one side holding a stiff conversation, their body language suggesting a mutual reluctance.

Emily threw a quick smile and shake of her head at Peter, which he interpreted with smothered relief, quickly throwing off his blanket and announcing that he was off to bed, testily fending off all offers of help.

'I'll just duck my head in once or twice in the night to make sure you're still all right,' Emily heard Ethan say. So he wasn't planning on staying at Carly's when he took her home, she thought with a pang of relief.

Ethan watched Peter limp away, then walked over to the other two protagonists. 'I'm sorry, Carly, this has been a bit of a disaster, hasn't it?' he said, smiling wryly into her beautiful face. 'You should have taken up my suggestion and stayed on without me.'

She looked at the glittering diamond bracelet on her wrist that Emily realised was a watch and began huskily, 'Well, we could still make the after-party—but no…' She shook her head, and not a strand of blonde hair escaped the perfect chignon. 'Naturally, you won't want to go out again—just in case. As a patron, though, I think I should go back to the theatre—so why don't I just call a taxi, to save you a trip?'

Emily almost liked her then, for being thoughtful enough not to insist on her escort fulfilling his duty, when she must secretly be annoyed that the medical emergency for which she had ruined her evening had proved to be such a petty incident.

Ethan made a swift call on his mobile to the corporate taxi service with whom he had an account, and while they were waiting he said to Carly, 'Perhaps you'll let me try to make it up to you with dinner tomorrow night?' He was exuding the kind of polished charm that Emily was more used to seeing from Dylan and she wasn't surprised to see Carly flutter her eyelash-extensions in gracious acceptance, but she was totally taken off guard as he continued impulsively, 'In fact, why don't we turn it into an occasion and make it a foursome?' He turned to include his startled brother in the invitation. 'Dylan and Emily can come with us—it's been an age since my brother and I dined out in each other's company, and we're all four in such diverse fields I'm sure it'll be fascinating fun.'

CHAPTER EIGHT

'IF THIS is your idea of fun, you need to see a psychiatrist,' said Emily three nights later as she observed Dylan and Carly move onto the small dance floor. In the dim light, Carly's white strapless dress looked almost luminous next to the jet-black of her partner's suit.

'Why, Emily, I thought you were enjoying yourself,' said Ethan, lounging beside her in his chair, watching her face in the flickering candlelight as a waiter discreetly removed the remains of their sumptuous meal.

'I am, but I don't know if they are,' she said, watching Carly stiffen, without losing an iota of poise, as Dylan put his arms around her and said something before drawing her into the sway of couples who were circling the floor to the romantic strains of a string quartet. Now it was Dylan who looked awkward as his partner's body blended instantly with the music, and she seemed to be taunting him with his lack of grace, the intensity of their conversation at odds with the relaxed mooching going on around them.

Carly and Dylan had been at polite loggerheads all night, taking opposing views on almost every topic, ignoring attempts by Emily to smooth things over while Ethan seemed for once content to relax and take a back seat, almost to encourage their bickering by his lack of assertiveness.

'Why aren't you out there dancing with her?' she asked as she saw Dylan rise swiftly to whatever challenge Carly had issued, jerking her closer and plunging himself into the mood of the music.

'Because Dylan asked her first,' Ethan replied lazily.

'She was waiting for *you* to ask.'

'She knows I have two left feet on the dance floor.'

'Still, you'd make the effort for *her*,' Emily couldn't help the faintly cutting emphasis, and hurried to disguise her slip, 'otherwise why bring us to a restaurant which features opera music and dancing as an essential part of its atmosphere?'

'The food?' murmured Ethan wryly. The restaurant's exclusivity and award-winning status had been the reason that the dinner-date had been postponed, even Ethan's considerable influence and greasing of palms not enough to gain them admittance in under a fortnight if it hadn't been for an unexpected cancellation.

'Well, yes, the food was rather fabulous,' admitted Emily. The Northern Italian cuisine had been impeccable, as had the silver service and the progression of expensive wines, although she noticed that Ethan, as their driver, had been very abstemious.

As if on cue, he signalled the hovering wine waiter to pour the last of a bottle of rich, ruby-red wine into her cut-crystal goblet.

'Oh, I don't think I should,' she murmured weakly as the wine began to flow, but the waiter only hesitated briefly before receiving a discreet nod from Ethan and continuing to pour her a generous half-glass.

Ethan leaned towards her, his chin on his hand, the low-burning candles in the centre of the table turning one side of his face into a saturnine mask, the other an intriguing dance of angles.

'Why not indulge yourself? You spend all day cooped up in that little studio with only a packed lunch, and in the evening you share Peter's restricted diet so he won't be tempted to sneak a helping of forbidden foods. You've earned a night of decadence.'

A whole night? Emily firmly quashed the errant thought. She was finding it difficult to cope with Ethan in this mood. In the last few days he had suddenly jettisoned his rock-crushing approach and opted for a more refined form of torture, each day succeeding in getting a little further under her frazzled skin with his silky-smooth courtesies. Emily knew she had Peter to thank for this apparent back-down. He was stonewalling his nephew and had sternly instructed him not to badger Emily with his questions.

'I think I've indulged myself a little too much already,' she said, giving him a slightly fuzzy smile, 'food *and* wine.'

'I noticed you mopping up your plate with your bread,' he teased, and saw the blush sweep up from the softly draped neckline of her floaty blue dress.

'I couldn't help it—that sauce was divine,' she said guiltily. 'I suppose I did come across as rather greedy.' She had noticed Carly had consumed only a small portion of each of her courses.

'I liked seeing you eat with such wonderful abandon,' he told her. 'You were in ecstasy with every bite. Dinner was a very sensual experience.'

She laughed, her hazy blue eyes not quite certain whether to be embarrassed or flattered. 'And then I went and ordered that chocolate dessert… I know I should have been like Carly, and had the fresh fruit and shaved ice—'

Ethan stroked the back of his fingers lightly over her rounded shoulder, bared by the self-tied straps of the halter-neck dress and down to the warm crease in the crook of her elbow.

'You could never be like Carly,' he murmured. 'She has angles, you have curves…soft, pretty, round curves that flow into one another with intriguing dips and hollows that make a man curious to explore each and every one…' His finger rubbed along the sensitive crease, finding the quick throb of her pulse on the inside of her elbow.

She took gulp of her wine, inadvertently trapping his finger instead of dislodging it as she had planned. 'Ethan—'

'You know, that dress is almost the exact shade of your eyes,' he decided, looking deeply into her flustered gaze.

'I—that's why I bought it,' she stammered, sitting back in her chair and dropping her hands in her lap to give her the excuse to shake off his intrusive touch. 'It's one of my favourites… I hope you can't still smell the smoke on it,' she blurted.

As a distraction it was a disaster. His smile warned her of her error as he dipped his head, inhaling the scent from her cleavage with a long, slow pull of his lungs, his chin brushing the slope of her breast, his hair lightly tickling the underside of her jaw.

Emily saw a middle-aged couple at another table watching them with raised eyebrows.

'Ethan, for goodness' sake!'

He raised his head, his eyes burning ice. 'Nothing but warm, lush woman with sexy undertones of sugar and spice and all things particularly nice.'

'And you're certainly slugs-and-snails at the moment,' she said shakily. 'You're supposed to be here with Carly. How would she feel if she saw you—saw you—?'

'Sniffing around you?' he mocked throatily. 'She won't. She's too preoccupied with snubbing my brother.'

Emily glanced over to the dance floor, where sure enough Carly was looking haughtily up at Dylan as he recklessly dipped her over his arm.

'You know he's in love with her,' she said flatly, having realised during the course of the evening what she was witnessing was not the behaviour of two relative strangers who were indifferent to each other. The pair had a history together and Dylan's obnoxious attitude was the adult equivalent of a little boy hitting his favourite girl to get her attention. There had been more than a strong hint of desperation in some of his sardonic remarks.

His eyebrows quirked as he followed her gaze. 'Is he?' he mused, entirely unalarmed. 'Or is it just that Dylan only wants what he can't have?'

'Like you?'

His head swung back and he grinned wolfishly. 'Why? Who is it you think I want that I can't have, Emily?'

She folded her arms, staring intently at the dancers, refusing to answer the loaded question.

'The woman I want I can have anywhere, any time, and she knows it as well as I do.' She felt a shocking warmth on her knee, the weight of his hand sliding slowly up under the filmy hem of her skirt to tease at the stretchy lace top of her stocking where it bit lightly into her silky inner thigh, sending quivering thrills streaking up into her heated core. She gasped, jolted into meeting his bland look. How could he sit there looking so calm and distinguished in his dark suit and pearl-grey shirt and tie while he was engaging in such wicked indecency? He would get them thrown out of the restaurant.

'Actually, I was thinking of Anna, your ex-fiancée,' she struck back cruelly, reaching under the shield of the tablecloth to remove the fingers moving tantalisingly close to their goal, and firmly crossing her legs to quell the dangerous excitement that threatened her fragile composure. 'Dylan told me all about your broken engagement.'

'Did he indeed? What else did he tell you about me?'

'Everything!'

Her terrifying declaration rebounded on her when he merely laughed.

'So, you must have been asking, then. Did you also ask him about Carly?' he guessed slyly. 'And did he tell you that they had an affair last year but he got cold feet when she started to hint at a more permanent arrangement?'

Emily's eyes widened and he smiled. 'I thought not. So, you see, his dog-in-the-manger act isn't going to cut much ice with her now. She's moved onto bigger game. He'll have to work a lot harder this time round, if he wants to take her away from me.'

He sat back and waited as Emily's brain clicked over the possibilities. 'I—is that why you two have being going out together?' she ventured tentatively. 'To make him jealous?'

He shrugged. It was his turn to be cruel. 'Would it make you feel better if I said yes?'

Her eyes flashed and he looked savagely pleased.

'Not pleasant, is it, Emily? To have burning questions that no one is willing to answer.'

She fiddled unconsciously with her heavy wineglass, her thick lashes lowered to reveal the burnished bronze eye shadow that emphasised the tilt of her eyes. Peter had shown her the reports that his local investigator had produced, but they were not as definitive as he had made out—there seemed more speculation, conjecture and hearsay than actual hard evidence. Her parents had evidently not responded to any inquiries, which, considering how elusive they were even to Emily, was not surprising, and she had been trying to get a call through to them to prove to Peter that his assumptions were wrong.

'Perhaps Carly will tell me,' she said stubbornly.

'I doubt it. I told her you were a gold-digging hussy, that if you didn't get your claws into Peter you'd be after Dylan or me.'

'You didn't!' she cried, almost spilling the last of the wine.

'At the time I thought you were,' he said in his own defence. 'In fact, the jury is still out on that one.'

'I'm not a gold-digger!'

'So you're admitting you're a hussy?'

She squeezed her crossed legs together and blushed. He had every right to think so, the way she had been carrying on.

'I'm just an ordinary woman trying to get on with her life.'

'If you think you're ordinary *you* need to see a psychiatrist,' he said drily, bringing their conversation full circle as Dylan and Carly returned to the table, accompanied by a distinct chill.

Emily thought the rest of the evening might prove to be awkward but over coffee and liqueurs Ethan finally roused himself to run interference and kept the talk ruthlessly general until Dylan asked Emily about the knuckle-bones story he'd heard from Peter. Even Carly seemed to be intrigued by the idea.

'You mean you grew up in a string of refugee camps?'

'We didn't always live in the camps themselves. Sometimes we were billeted or lived in nearby villages.'

'I hadn't realised you travelled with them,' frowned Ethan. 'Wasn't it rather dangerous, taking a baby into emergency situations?'

'Mum and Dad didn't start doing emergency relief until I got to school age and came back to live with my grandparents. Up until then they took postings with long-term aid programmes, which were usually in stable areas, relatively speaking.'

'Relative to what?' demanded Ethan.

'Well, where they are now, I suppose. I mean, I saw a lot of hardship and ugly sights, but I was a kid so I never thought too deeply about what it all meant. I was more worried about having to eat some of the food!' Emily's joking reference glossed lightly over the years of gastrointestinal upsets she had endured in areas where clean water and hygienic living conditions had been in extremely short supply. Only Ethan seemed to acknowledge the false cheer in her voice with a sharp look.

'It must have been a fascinating experience, all that travel and adventure. And yet you never wanted to follow your parents into aid work?' asked Carly, and the edge of criticism in her voice made Emily suddenly remember that this woman had been told she was a gold-digger.

'I think I got all the travel and adventure out of my system early on,' she said. 'It takes a special kind of person to choose to live the way that my parents do—'

'You mean, as altruists?'

'I think she means as adrenalin junkies,' said Ethan drily, once more confounding Emily with his intuition.

'But very *altruistic* adrenalin junkies,' she pointed out with a smile.

Carly clearly didn't appreciate their humour. 'I think people like that are wonderful!'

'Yes, they are. Just very hard to live up to.'

She was accorded a condescending look. 'I'm sure you do your best.'

'I'm reliably informed that doing my best isn't good enough.'

'How cruel.'

'Yes, wasn't it?' said Emily, with a smug look at Ethan. 'Anyway, I much prefer staying in one place these days.'

'I take it you mean Peter's,' commented Ethan.

'Hey, what's happening about that, anyway?' said Dylan. 'Have you heard anything from your insurance company?'

Emily sighed. 'Now they're admitting it was fireworks— some sort of rocket breaking the studio window. The only question is whether it was deliberate or accidental. We had had several incidents of hooligans firing them off from cars around the neighbourhood at Guy Fawkes—'

'So you'll get your payout soon,' said Dylan.

'I hope so,' said Emily, doubt sounding in her voice. There was still the business of the indemnity value to work out. 'The good news is that my house won't have to be entirely demolished, just parts of it. The rest can be rebuilt, once it's been strengthened.'

'Why don't you let me sort it out for you?' said Ethan abruptly as they all rose to leave. 'I'm used to dealing with insurance hassles in the building industry. I'll give that bloke Tremaine a call and see what I can find out.' His voice suggested it was already a foregone conclusion.

'Good idea. Sic Ethan onto 'em,' advised Dylan. 'He'll sink his teeth into them for you and shake something loose. He's a real bulldog when it comes to getting answers.'

Didn't she know it!

'No, really I—'

'Oh, come on, Emily, let him do it—you don't keep a dog and bark yourself!' Dylan gave a theatrical little howl that earned him a sharp nudge from Carly.

'Dogs seem to be the theme of the night,' murmured Emily, giving Ethan a sidelong glance. 'I didn't know I kept one.'

'Woof, woof,' he said, his deep, resonating voice startling the *maître d'* as he handed back his platinum credit card.

Maybe the two brothers weren't so different from each other after all, thought Emily, exchanging a surprisingly friendly roll of the eyes with Carly.

Dylan's good humour lasted until they got into the car, and he discovered that Ethan was going to drop him off with Emily first before driving Carly back into town to her cliff-top villa. He took his revenge by whispering all the way home in Emily's unwilling ear, telling some irresistibly funny jokes, and making much of their apparently intimate conversation.

Emily, aware of Ethan's cool eyes using the rear-vision mirror with a meticulous regularity that would render him a pin-up with the traffic safety boys, squirmed uncomfortably in the knowledge of what he must be seeing, while Carly haughtily appeared not to notice, turning up the classical music station on the radio to drown out the whispers and giggles floating over from the darkness in the back seat.

The laughter was abruptly cut off as Dylan stood under the portico of the house and watched the red lights at the rear of the BMW flare briefly at the gates of the house before the headlights swept into the darkness along Ridge Road.

He withdrew his keys from his pocket and unlocked the front door for Emily, then, muttering under his breath, he spun on his heel and started walking across the drive.

'What are you doing?' called Emily softly, suffering her own form of depression. After all, Ethan had never actually *confirmed* her inference that he and Carly were merely acting a charade for Dylan's benefit. And perhaps he thought she had been encouraging Dylan's behaviour in the back seat, rather than simply enduring it.

'Going out,' he said, jingling his keys, and she realised he was making for the Porsche, parked in the inky shadow of the garage.

Emily ran after him, grabbing the sleeve of his jacket.

'You can't drive,' she told him. 'You've been drinking.'

He gave a short crack of disbelieving laughter and she snatched the keys out of his hand. 'Hey!'

'I'm serious, Dylan.'

'Then *you* drive me.'

Drive the Porsche? She had a wistful image of herself at the wheel, zipping past Ethan on the motorway. 'I've probably had more to drink than you,' she said.

'I want to go clubbing,' he said sullenly, making a swipe for the keys. 'Hand them over!'

'Dylan, you told me the Porsche is only leased because you couldn't afford to buy one. If you crash it you'll *have* to pay for it. And are you really in the mood to party? Or are you just going to go to a bar somewhere and get smashed—or drive over to Carly's and sit outside in your car, brooding?'

'Huh!' he muttered.

Emily didn't know which option he was choosing, but at least his flare of temper seemed to have died down.

'If you have to go somewhere, call for a taxi,' she said, turning him back in the direction of the house.

'No, I may as well just go to bed,' he said, stomping into the hall. 'What a bitch!'

'I hope you're not referring to me.'

'I was talking about life in general…and *her*.'

Emily was beginning to have reluctant sympathy for Carly. Dylan was a temperamental handful, in love with a richer, classier, older woman. His masculine pride was on the line and, even though he was gasping his last, he was refusing to admit he was hooked, gaffed and landed.

She watched in relief as he vanished into his room, hoping he didn't have a second set of keys hidden in there.

Glancing at her watch and mentally juggling time zones, she detoured to the telephone in the lounge and waited for the minute hand to tick around to the half hour before she punched in the number that she had been given. It took four re-dials before she got through and even then the interference on the satellite phone at the other end was considerable, and she wasn't able to recognise the language of the garbled voice. Then she hit a clean patch and a new voice came on the line.

'Mum? Mum, is that you?'

The phone roared, then mumbled, then dropped out completely, but then she heard loud and clear, at least for the first four words: 'Emily? Right on time…Almost missed y…Dad says 'hi'…What's happening, Em? I haven't forgotten your birthday again, have I?' A familiar, faraway, tinny laugh that she hadn't heard for several months.

'No, it's not for another six months, Mum. How are you both…?'

She struggled on with the usual set of commonplaces for a few more minutes, and then, conscious that the reception at the other end was getting worse not better, hurriedly told her mother about the fire.

'Too bad, Em…wish…help…absolute chaos here at the moment…need money?'

It was always chaos, wherever they were. They thrived on it. And she knew very well that most of their money they gave away to people a lot more needy than Emily, who at least had food to eat, and a blanket at night and didn't risk rape or mutilation or worse every time she ventured away from the perimeter of the house. She would feel as guilty as sin if she pleaded poverty over those to whom mere poverty would be a luxury.

'No, no, I'm fine, I'm managing. But, Mum, a funny thing happened…' She haltingly told her mother about Peter Nash taking her in, and his fantastic notion that she might be adopted, pausing between running phrases for the worst of the white noise to fade.

She thought they had been cut off when there was a long, blank pause, then she almost dropped the telephone when her mother's voice came in thin little bursts. 'Oh, dear…I wish…see you…. It's complicated, Em…little point in your…so we thought…legal…adopted…not really…'

There was more but it was such a word soup that Emily wasn't sure she could make any sense of it, not when her whole brain was screaming in denial. 'What's that, Mum? I can't hear you. Am I adopted or aren't I?' She panicked as the white noise thickened, almost completely swamping her mother's next sentences.

'You're breaking up, Mum. Just tell me yes or no. That's all you need to say. Just *Yes* or *No!*'

'Sorry…ring you…soon…promise…truck…we can get clear air…yes…YES!'

Emily didn't know how long she sat in the darkened room, staring at the dead phone.

Yes?

She was *adopted?* A burning liquid rose in her throat and she swallowed it back.

No. She *couldn't* be. Surely not. Why wouldn't they ever have told her? As a child…or when she turned eighteen…or any other time in the past twenty-six years? Because she was the daughter of a teenage drug addict? There was no great stigma in that these days. That *couldn't* have been what her mother had been saying. They had probably been talking totally at cross purposes.

Her eyes felt hot and dry. If anything she was *worse* off, even more uncertain than before she had made the call. The bad reception had flattened all emotional tone but her mother's words had expressed regret rather than shock that she should ask the question. And what was so complicated? Her alcohol-slowed brain scurried round and round in ever-diminishing circles.

She looked at her watch, astonished to see that half an hour had passed. It was too late to call again. The window of satellite opportunity in such a remote area was extremely small, and who knew when she could successfully draw all the threads together to arrange another call? She would just have to hope that her mother would be able to get access to another phone and ring back soon.

She heard the faint hum of an engine and jumped to her feet. Was that Ethan back? Oh, she couldn't bear it if he found her waiting here in the dark. He might think she was waiting for him. He might take her in his arms and it would all come bursting out, all her festering doubts and untidy emotions.

God, she might even be drunk and vulnerable enough to blurt out the fact that she was falling in love with him…and *then*, just to complete the farce, she could hit him with the fact that she could well be his uncle's granddaughter!

She crept along to her room and undressed in the dark, afraid the light under the door would give her away as she heard Ethan enter the house.

She slept, but she woke up several times with nightmares. Not the smoky new nightmares but the old ones, from her childhood, the nightmares of running, running after a truck that was leaving, choking in a trail of dust as she tried to run faster and faster to catch her mother and father reaching out from the tailgate. But the faster she ran, the further the truck moved away until it was only a tiny dot in the distance and she was left behind alone.

Finally, just before dawn, she got up and went along to the studio. There at least was a world of order and certainty, where everything could be put back to rights with a good clean and the right kind of glue.

If only people's shattered emotions could be as easily glued back together, she thought as she double-checked the pieces of the dismantled blue and white vase that had been soaked in detergent, rinsed and dried, the iron-stained areas treated with a reducing agent and a soiled crack swabbed with hydrogen peroxide.

Now came the fiddly task of filling the cleaned rivet-holes and Emily forced herself to concentrate on nothing else as she mixed up the epoxy resin, which she tinted to the background colour of the vase, having taken the care to do a number of tests before she had finally settled on the correct shade.

By the time she had done several hours' work she felt much more like herself—whoever that was! she thought with gallows humour—and sufficiently hungry to realise she might be able to eat breakfast after all. She had already decided not to tell Peter about her phone call—she could offer to pay for it later. There seemed no point in getting his hopes up until she could tell him something more concrete. In the cold light of day the call seemed nightmarishly unreal and she found it difficult to remember the sequence of the disjointed conversation.

Since the dining room was empty she concluded that Peter had already breakfasted and the earlier rumble that had impinged on her concentration had been Dylan and Ethan leaving for work. Moving on to the kitchen she discovered Mrs Cooper muttering darkly with her head in the oven and quickly helped herself to cereal and juice and took it out onto the verandah to eat in the sunshine.

Towards lunchtime when she looked in on Peter in his office she was able to give him a cheerful smile and, remembering the message the previous day about the house, asked apologetically if he would mind if Jeff ran her down later to start to organise the site clean-up and make lists of everything she would need to have ready when her money came through.

'Oh, no need for you to bother with that any more,' said Peter, linking his arm with hers and walking her outside. 'It'll be much more convenient for both of us if you can just drive yourself.'

'But, Peter, I—' She came to a dead stop as she stared at the jaunty little yellow car parked in front of the portico, a shiny three-door hatchback with a dealer's sticker on the rear window. 'What's this?'

But she feared she knew. Peter nudged her over to open the driver's door releasing the unmistakable 'brand new' aroma of plastic and chemicals, and indicated the set of keys in the ignition.

'It's gassed up and all ready to go,' he said. 'I know you hate asking for every little thing. Now you don't have to bother Jeff or I when you want to go anywhere. You can just hop in and tootle off whenever you like.'

This wasn't a 'little' thing. Her blue eyes scolded him. 'Peter, we've been through all this—you can't just give me a car—'

'I'm not *giving* it to you,' he said, looking wounded. 'I've bought a second car, a little runabout for myself, that's all, and I'm lending it to you while you're here.'

'A runabout!' she exclaimed. 'Where are you thinking of running about to?' Heavens, she was beginning to sound like Ethan!

His white tufted eyebrows lifted in dignified reproach. 'I do have a licence, you know, Emily, I just find it convenient to let Jeff do most of the driving. But this'll be handy for me when Jeff's not around.'

She eyed him sceptically. 'If I say no will you take it back to the dealer?'

'Of course not,' he said stoutly. 'I told you, it's bought and paid for. It can just sit there and we'll roust Jeff out to do your driving for you, if that's how you want to go on.'

She sighed and he pinched off a triumphant smile. 'I don't know what Ethan's going to say,' she murmured, touching the pristine paintwork.

'What can he say? He's got two cars, a four-wheel drive *and* a helicopter. He can't begrudge me a second string to my bow.'

Oh, yes, he could. She hesitated. 'I hope this isn't just because of—you know, because you hope I might be your granddaughter—' she began awkwardly.

'It's because I'm a rich man and I can afford to indulge my own whims,' he said firmly.

'Well…all right, then.' Her objections to his happy fiction wilted in the face of her dawning excitement. She had never driven a brand-new car before. And it would mean she could get a lot more done with regard to her house. 'But it's just a loan,' she reminded them both as she got in and started the engine.

By the time she turned back into the drive it was late afternoon and she was very pleased to have lined up a firm of commercial cleaners who would move in to the salvageable part of the house as soon as her funding came through. She had also been to the supermarket and chemist, and bought herself a few intimate essentials and extra studio supplies. Having full room and board meant she was able to eke out her small store of savings, which would have otherwise been swallowed up by now in living expenses and the myriad costs involved in pursuing her claim. It had been also essential for her to buy a new mobile phone to re-establish Quest Restorations with a working number, and although she had bought the cheapest on the market it had still made a dent in her limited budget.

As she passed the mirror in the hallway she noticed that she was also well overdue for a haircut, but as a non-essential that would have to wait, unless she decided to get creative herself with the scissors.

After dropping her purchases off in her room she saw the door to the room where Rose's collection was displayed was ajar and, thinking Peter might be in there communing with his memories, she slipped inside only to see Ethan in shirt-sleeves and work boots, standing looking into one of the open-fronted cabinets.

She thought she had been silent, but Ethan said without looking around: 'This is it, isn't it?'

Mastering her skittering heart, she moved up to his shoulder and found herself looking at a very familiar object.

'Yes, that's the pilgrim flask.'

'Pretty. Can I pick it up, or do I need gloves?'

She shuddered. 'No gloves—too much chance of it slipping through your fingers. Bare hands are fine—as long as they're clean.'

'Yes, Nanny.' He flipped his hands over for her inspection and picked up the porcelain, handling it with a confident delicacy that sent a tingle down her spine.

'What incredibly detailed decoration—what is this, a dragon?'

'A water dragon—there's one on both sides,' she pointed out, showing him the blue painting on the reverse, 'and this pattern represents breaking waves and rocks—and here's the clouds and flowering shrubs.'

'They pack a lot of story into a small space.'

'That shows the talent of the artist, one of the reasons it's so valuable. It's not only history, it's great art.' She watched him carefully set the flask back on the shelf, her voice filled with self-castigation. 'Looking back, I can't believe what I dared to do. *Anything* could have happened—'

'Anything did,' said Ethan, turning around. 'You took a risk and it paid off.'

'I'm not generally a risk-taker,' she protested.

His pale eyes glinted. 'I don't think you know yourself half as well as you think you do,' he murmured.

If only he knew how truly he spoke! Swallowing down a little hiccup of hysteria, Emily quickly focused her attention back on the shelves of porcelain and gave Ethan a sketchy tour of the contents. Then they looked at the pieces the appraiser had singled out for his thumbs-down, and Ethan studied some of the Meissen dinnerware she had formerly repaired, looking in vain for the evidence of restoration.

'Usually if you can't see any surface defect and you want to know if there's a break you can find out with a flick test,' said Emily, setting a dish down on a display table and tapping it with her fingernail. 'If there's no crack it should resonate with a "ting", otherwise you'll get a dull sound.'

They listened to the pure sing of the ceramic.

'Hence the origin of the phrase to "ring true",' said Ethan, his eyes moving speculatively over her face. He tapped her lightly on the jaw and cocked his head at the soft thud of his finger on the bone. 'Does that mean you're cracked?'

She was certainly crazy, she thought as she looked up into his brutally attractive face. Crazy for him. And her heart would be in serious danger of cracking if she couldn't work out some way to be with him in spite of the swirl of secrets that had engendered his wary mistrust. 'It doesn't work with people,' she said huskily.

'More's the pity. I guess that means I have to find another way to tap your hidden depths…' His arms slid around her pliant waist and he began to lower his head when a delicious buzz shot into her groin from his pressing hip. He groaned, reaching into his jeans pocket. 'Sorry, my phone…I've been waiting for this call…' And she had to settle for a quick tousle of her curls rather than the long, lush kiss of her desires.

His voice dropped into brisk and urgent technical jargon as he strode out of the room and not long after she heard a car leave, presuming that he had been called back to the office.

Hunger pangs reminded her that lunch had been an apple and a handful of Vegemite crackers given to her by her neighbour, who had wandered over for a gossip when she had seen Emily dealing with the parade of tradesman she had invited to provide free quotes.

While she was in the kitchen making herself a sandwich, Mrs

Cooper showed her the dinner roast, surrounded with vegetables, which she had put in the oven to turn on with an automatic timer, and pointed out the snapped beans that would only have to be popped into the microwave.

She was crossing back through the hall, finishing the last of her sandwich, when she met Peter coming out of his office fare-welling a short, sandy-haired man with black-rimmed glasses, whom he introduced as Andrew Robinson, his lawyer.

The lawyer switched his slim briefcase to his left side in order to shake her hand, his green eyes chilly as he murmured her name.

She found out why when Peter, as if to mitigate the impact of his lawyer's radiating disapproval, blurted out that he had just signed a codicil adding Emily to his will.

Emily blanched, her sandwich congealing into a doughy brick in her stomach. First the car. Now this. 'Peter, you can't do this—'

'I can and I have,' he said proudly. 'I wish everyone would stop telling me that I don't know what I'm doing.' He cast a con-demning look at his lawyer.

'But...for goodness sake! We don't know anything yet,' she said frantically. All she could think of was Ethan's reaction. 'You can't change your will on the basis of some vague *hope,* and that's all it is at this stage, Peter. Nothing's been proven, and maybe never will—'

'I told him he would be wise to wait for a DNA test before making any hasty decisions,' Andrew Robinson put in dourly, 'but he insisted that he didn't want to wait.'

'What if I popped off tomorrow,' said Peter, 'and left you with nothing?'

'But I don't *expect* anything. I don't *want* anything more than you've given me already. Even if I *did* turn out by some *fantastic* coincidence to be your granddaughter, you don't have to do this.'

She just wanted to be plain Emily Quest, restoration artist, someone that Ethan could respect, trust, fall in love with...

'It wouldn't be such an unlikely coincidence as you think,' said Peter gruffly. 'When the Quest name was thrown up, and I found out what you did, I was the one who suggested that Rose get Quest Restorations to start handling the repair jobs she had been giving to another company.'

His behind-the-scene manipulation only seemed to make it worse. So much for his wanting to keep his wife away from his secret!

'Peter, you haven't even told your *family* yet. If you're so certain of all this, why haven't you told them what you told me? It isn't fair to ambush them like this. How can you expect them to understand?'

'They don't have to understand, they just have to accept it. A man's last will and testament is his own—'

'Understand what? What's going on?' Ethan appeared from the lounge, pocketing his phone, frowning at the sight of the lawyer and Emily's frozen figure. 'Peter?' His eyes moved to the lawyer's briefcase and his gaze shuttered. 'Andrew? What is this?'

No one spoke, and then the dam inside Emily burst.

'Your uncle has decided to change his will in my favour. You're out and I'm in!' she announced with wild inaccuracy. 'And because I'm nothing but a wretched little gold-digger, of course I'm utterly thrilled about it!'

'Changed his will?' His voice was neutral, his face solid granite as he said carefully: 'Well, that's his prerogative, I suppose—'

'Aren't you going to ask why?' she cut in shrilly, infuriated by his restraint, when she could see the gathering storm in his eyes. He would save all that for her. He would blame her, she knew it!

'I don't have to—'

She gave a sardonic laugh. 'Oh, yes, you do—believe me, you're going to want to know.' She swung around on Peter, for the first time bitterly angry with his meddling, with his attempt to rearrange his mistakes of the past by arbitrarily rearranging her entire future. 'You tell him,' she said fiercely. 'You tell him who you think I am, or I will. I'm tired of being the pawn in a game I never chose to play. I'm not going to be the keeper of anyone's dirty little secrets any more. I'm not sure where I belong, but right now it's certainly not in this house!'

And with that she turned and ran out past her bedroom, out to the studio she couldn't open because she had locked it and didn't have the key. Locked out of her only sanctuary—except that sanctuary really wasn't hers, either. Eyes blind with tears, she slumped against the door, arms around her middle, trying to shore herself up against the pain of her crumbling dreams.

CHAPTER NINE

EMILY lifted her face into the wind, feeling the salt spray sting her face, dashing away the last of the tear tracks on her cheeks.

'I can't believe I'm doing this!' she yelled, gripping the rail and bending her knees to ride out the bumps, the orange life-jacket protecting most of her tee shirt but her white cotton capri pants plastered damply to her thighs.

'Doing what?' shouted Dylan from the boat's cockpit as he turned the wheel and increased the throttle, pumping more power through the twin engines so that the white hull lifted to skim across the tops of the choppy waves in a wide, curving turn towards the green slopes of Waiheke Island rising from the waters of the Gulf.

'Running away!' She turned to look at him over her shoulder from her perch on the prow of the sleek launch, her hair lashing across her eyes and whipping at her cheeks.

'I do it all the time,' Dylan called, his wide grin slashing his face under the wraparound sunglasses. The wind ripped the rest of her words away and Emily turned back into the wind, enjoying the relentless physical buffeting as an escape from the mental roughing-up she had given herself.

If it had been anyone other than Dylan who had found her sobbing her heart out against the locked studio door she would still be in captivity, probably locked in yet another row, or miserable round of question-and-answer, but he had driven up in his Porsche, taken one look at her blotchy, woebegone face and des-

perate eyes, and bundled her into his passenger seat for a thera-
peutic getaway.

'Is Ethan in there?' he said, jerking his head towards the
house. When she nodded, her eyes brimming with fresh tears, he
restarted the engine and ordered her to buckle up.

The actor renting his apartment had leased a jet-boat, he
informed her as he headed out towards the eastern string of
beaches, and he had asked Dylan to pick it up from the marina
and take it out for a test-run before he delivered it to its temporary moorings near the waterfront apartment block.

'You can be my navigator,' he said.

'I don't know anything about boats.' Emily sniffed miserably
into the tissue he had produced from the glove compartment.

'You can be lookout, then,' he said. 'I'll stuff you up in the
crow's nest. But you have to stop crying because I don't want to
crash into any icebergs.'

She laughed soggily at that, grateful that he wasn't asking any
awkward questions, though she was sure she had heard him
curse his brother under his breath as he'd put the car into gear.

'Did you go out again last night?' she asked as she dabbed
at her eyes.

'No, ma'am, I stayed home like I was told and did my
brooding in the safety of my own bed. I guess I was being pretty
obvious, huh? I was acting like a jerk in the car—no wonder she
despises me for being immature—'

'I don't think she despises you—'

But Dylan was off and running, and since misery loved
company Emily listened to his romantic woes and commiserated
with his angry frustration.

'Hell, I know deep down that Ethan wouldn't cut me out with
her, not unless he was really in love with her—which he isn't.
We've never gone for the same kind of girl. Carly is too highly
polished for Ethan, he likes a bit of rough—uh--' he almost bit
off his tongue when he realised what he'd said '—er—no
offence, Emily.'

'None taken,' she said mildly. At least he had put them together in his mind. She knew that initially he had picked her as a way to divide his brother's attention, but he must have figured out by now that there was a lot more going on than met the eye.

'I—didn't mean—I mean, he's an earthy kind of a guy…' It was the first time she had ever heard Dylan stammer she and found it rather endearing. 'He prefers a challenge— Anything too easy for him is a turn-off—uh—'

'Quit while you're ahead, Dylan,' she told him wryly.

'I think I will,' he said, relieved to return to his favourite subject, and Emily realised as he outlined his dark plan for Carly's ultimate downfall that she was listening to the death throes of his masculine independence.

'Ahoy there! Any iceberg alerts?' he called, and she felt the salt tightness on her skin as she smiled and shook her head. Holding the rail, she moved hand-over-hand to scramble back down beside him in the cockpit.

'Nothing like a bumpy ride to blow away the cobwebs,' he laughed.

'It does look as if the wind is picking up a bit,' said Emily, looking out at the increasing number of white-caps. She glanced up at the sky. It was still sunny, but high cloud was scudding in from the west, over the landmass of greater Auckland.

'It'll be more sheltered once we get around the leeward side of the island. The mooring at Oneroa should be pretty calm.'

'Mooring? Dylan—I thought we were just coming out for a run,' she said anxiously.

'We are. A run to Waiheke and back. With a leisurely beer in between. I've got a key to Ethan's place, and we know it's empty. We can raid his fridge and you can trash his wardrobe!'

'Dylan!'

'Oh, come on.' His teeth flashed like a shark's. 'Aren't you the least curious to have a peek? He'll never know we've been there, I promise. We can glide in and out like the proverbial ghosts. His house is right on the water, so we can zip right up alongside his jetty, whip upstairs for drinkies, and be back into town for tea with a star of stage and screen.'

Emily's arms were goose-pimpling. 'We really shouldn't. It's invading his privacy.'

'Privacy, smivacy. He wouldn't have given me the key and the security code if he didn't expect me to drop in whenever I felt like it. He made you cry, for God's sake—don't you want to smear some of your tears on his pillow to haunt him?'

He took her slightly stunned silence at his morbidly fascinating train of thought for agreement and throttled back the engine as they nosed into the bay.

'He didn't exactly make me cry,' admitted Emily, and while they tied up the boat to the jetty and trekked up the long wooden staircase to the concrete-and-glass house tucked in amongst the trees she told him about his uncle's bombshell, bracing herself for his furious reaction.

'Cool,' was all he said, punching in a security code on the solid hardwood slab that was the front door. 'I've always wanted a sister.'

'I'm not a *sister!*' she screeched, recoiling at the thought of such a close relationship with Ethan, and hugely put out by his casual acceptance of what to her had been a monumental blow.

'I meant a metaphorical sister,' he said, motioning her to leave her wet canvas slip-ons beside his boat shoes on the mat, and leading her into a huge white room with polished wood floors and a wall of windows looking out across the water.

She followed him absently into the white open-plan kitchen, frowning over exactly what their relationship could be labelled, realising it didn't fit into any convenient box.

'I'd be…well, the granddaughter of your uncle by marriage, so no relation at all, really. And, anyway, I'm sure it's all nonsense! The point you seem to be missing is—Peter has already put me in his *will*. Aren't you upset? God knows what Ethan is thinking now!' she finished in a tragic burst.

'So rather than stay and ask him, you elope with me. Good

strategy,' said Dylan, handing her a chilled bottle of Belgian beer from the double-doored refrigerator.

'We didn't *elope*,' she said, unscrewing the top of the beer and feeling the foaming icy brew numb the slight soreness at the back of her throat.

'So you won't marry me and make me rich. Sigh!'

'I thought you were already rich,' she said.

'I'm not very good at handling money,' he admitted. 'I'm like Dad in that respect—easy come easy go. But, like him, I always seem to bounce back. Well, if not you, I'll obviously have to marry some other rich woman, preferably someone who is a whiz at finances and snooty enough to keep me on the straight and narrow. Now, who do I know who can fit the bill?' he asked with an incorrigible grin. He finished half his beer in a single draught and opened the fridge again.

'Hey, Goldilocks—want to snoop around and try out Papa Bear's bed? I'm not one for porridge but this caviare looks good and there's several sorts of dips and spreads. I'm going to make up some canapés to put a lining on my stomach for the return trip…'

There spoke the difference in their upbringing and status, thought Emily in wry amusement as she wandered away—she would have made up some crackers, to Dylan they were canapés.

The rest of the house was as large and as beautifully laid out as the living areas, the furnishings classic and simple, the white walls soaring high to timbered ceilings with open beams, and slivered skylights punched in at odd angles to add to the total impression of airy lightness. There were two luxurious, white marble full bathrooms, and an *en suite* adjoining the bedroom that obviously belonged to the master, because there was a large vase of marmalade-orange roses on the bureau under the window and out through the slatted wooden blinds she saw an enchanting miniature rose garden, formally laid out with low box hedges, paved paths and a sleek wooden bench facing a small classical fountain.

She did sit on the side of Ethan's bed, although she didn't quite dare to lie down, and hugged his pillow to her breast, snuggling her nose into its crisp white pure cotton cover and catching just the tiniest whiff of his scent. Would she ever get to come back here again? Perhaps she was making a mountain out of a molehill, as Dylan implied. Or would this latest deception be the last straw as far as Ethan was concerned—representing the dull ring of an unsound relationship?

Before she could start bawling again she took her half empty bottle of rapidly warming beer back out to the lounge where Dylan was lying on the couch watching cable sports on the large flatscreen television mounted on the wall, drinking beer and munching his way through a plate of canapés.

'Dylan, don't you think we should be going?' she said, frowning at the greying seas out in the bay. How long had she been mooning in the bedroom? 'It's totally clouded over now, and the waves are beginning to get up.'

But Dylan had frozen with a caviare cracker halfway to his mouth. 'Uh-oh.'

'What's the matter?' she said, pouring the rest of her beer down the sink. 'Bad fish?'

He hit the off button on the remote control and sat up, tilting his head in a listening attitude.

'What uh-oh?' she said, crossing over towards him, and then she heard it too. She looked out the window at the sky, empty of everything but clouds and the occasional diving sea-bird, but she could definitely hear a helicopter. 'Dylan, what uh-oh?'

She went to peer nervously out another window. 'That's not what I think it is, is it? I mean, plenty of people on Waiheke have helicopters, don't they?'

'Sure, dozens,' said Dylan unconvincingly, quickly gathering up his debris.

'And there's an airfield, isn't there? Maybe it's a commercial chopper—or a rescue helicopter!' she said brightly.

'That would work for me,' muttered Dylan as he whipped open the cupboard under the sink and stuffed his rubbish into the kitchen bin.

'Ethan's helicopter wasn't at Peter's—how could it be him?' she panicked.

'There are such things as telephones, you know,' said Dylan, and then looked so innocent that a light bulb exploded in her head.

'You phoned him!'

'No, I didn't!'

She remembered him doing something furtive on the way over and now realised what it was. 'Then you sent him a text from the boat!' she accused and he looked sheepish.

'Force of habit,' he said weakly. 'I usually buzz him to let him know when I'm calling in. You know, just in case I trip off the silent alarm or something…and so he or I don't barge in on any—er—embarrassing scenes…'

She was going to accuse him of lying through his teeth, but she was diverted by the outrage of his last comment. 'You mean when either of you bring women here!'

By now the helicopter was directly overhead and she glimpsed the distinctive yellow livery as it heeled around to the landing circle down by the jetty.

'I'd better go and see what he wants.' Dylan was out the door like a rat down a drainpipe.

'We *know* what he wants—' she yelled after him, and he paused on the steps to grin back up at her.

'You mean you hope you do!'

'Your head on a pike—traitor!'

She slammed the door and went to spy out the window. The brothers met at the halfway point on the flight of steps and she expected to see a sharp altercation, and then both of them coming up towards her, but instead, after a brief exchange of words, Dylan bounded on down to the jetty and untied the boat. Slinging on his life-jacket, he jumped into the driving seat and was smoothly powering away across the wicked chop.

Heart beating nervously in her breast, Emily waited for the door to slam open and battle to commence, but instead there was a long wait for a very soft knock.

Running shaking hands through her curls and plucking her damp pants away from her legs, but resigned to looking like a wind-blown scarecrow, Emily tentatively opened the door.

Ethan had one hand propped on the side of the door-frame, his other hooked into his leather belt, one hip canted, the other leg bent casually at the knee. In the khaki shirt and jeans, with slight shadows under the ice-clear eyes, he looked like an everyday Joe, home from a hard day's work. His long, pale feet were bare, his scuffed brown boots sitting on the mat, looming over her dainty slip-ons.

'Ethan…'

'I forgot my key,' he said wryly, and, after a pause during which neither moved, 'May I come in?'

She blushed, colour moving swiftly into her bloodless cheeks as she almost tripped in her haste to make way. 'Of course…it's your house, after all.'

'I'm glad you clarified that,' he said, brushing past her. 'Because for a moment there I had my doubts.'

'Ethan—'

He forestalled her breathless rush of explanations, slowly revolving in the centre of the living space. 'You like it?'

Her bare toes curled nervously to grip the polished floor-boards, which seemed to tilt under her feet as she watched him spread his arms, his shirt pulling taut against the muscles of his chest, his short sleeves cutting into the strong biceps. 'Like what?'

'The house?'

'Yes, yes, of course, it's beautiful, especially the—'

'The what?' he said, dropping his arms.

She bit her lip, hoping he thought she'd been wandering around outside. 'The rose garden.'

'Ah, that…' He prowled back towards her and she found her hands twisting together, her blue eyes enlarged with confusion and regret, her soft mouth barely under control as he came to a halt barely a breath away. 'What do you have to say for yourself?'

She knew he wasn't asking about roses. 'Ethan, I'm sorry…'

But he wasn't interested in apologies. 'Don't ever do that again,' he said with measured softness.

'Run away with Dylan?' she joked weakly, but his face remained sternly intent, his body relaxed yet spring-loaded with inner tension.

'Make assumptions about me.'

'But—Peter—he *did* tell you—'

'He told me—he and Andrew—the whole, long, gory story. He showed me all his so-called reports. But whichever which way you cut it, you are not in any way related to *me*,' he said with a ruthless emphasis.

'I never claimed—'

'You think I don't know that!' he said, showing the first flash of his repressed fury. 'No matter who or what you are, you think I don't know that all this has arisen from Uncle Peter's own un-resolved guilt? I *know* you didn't approach him trying to pass yourself off as his granddaughter, because no one even knew he damned well had one! Yet you immediately assumed I would jump to the wrong conclusions. I thought you knew me better than that by now. Apparently you need a fresh lesson.' The icy fire in his eyes changed to another kind of heat as he made a dismissive gesture with his hand.

'But I don't want to talk about any of that now—I'm done with talking.' His eyes locked with hers and his voice deepened and slowed to an explicit, sexy, drawl—all the tension in him focused on a single goal.

'What I want is for the rest of the world to go away and let us concentrate on what's really important.' He moved from close-ness to intimacy, still without touching her, but stroking her all over with that wonderful voice of gravelled velvet: 'I want to make love to you, here and now, in my house, openly and alone…no helpful relatives, no pesky interruptions, no tortured revelations…just you and I, showing ourselves how good we can make each other feel…'

He cupped her face in both of his hands and brought his

mouth slowly down to part over hers, sinking them both into the luxury of a luscious, languorous, blissfully uninterrupted kiss. All Emily's cares and worries were wiped away in an instant, overtaken by warm and wondrous delight, her aching uncertainties absorbed by a sense of rightness, of glorious belonging…

The thickening of the clouds outside the window was matched by a growing tempest within as their swaying bodies broke and reformed with passionate hunger, excitement outstripping the initial slow, sensuous coming together. With a breathtakingly quick motion, Ethan peeled the scoop-necked yellow tee shirt over her head and threw it on the floor, retaking her mouth as he pushed his flattened hands down into the elasticated sides of her capri pants to rake them down her silky-smooth legs, lifting her out of the pooled fabric, and setting her gently down on her slender feet again so that he could enjoy the sight of her honey-gold body trembling for his touch. This time her bra and barely there panties actually matched and he stroked the transparent front panel of the deep red, hi-cut bikini and murmured thickly, 'Did you wear these just for me?'

She looked down and discovered that the lace motif his finger was tracing was a pattern of roses swirling down between her legs. If she had, it was an unconscious choice, but then, so much of her reaction to him was beyond her conscious control…

'Of course I did,' she encouraged him wantonly, arching her back so that her breasts lifted in their fragile bondage of scalloped lace.

She shivered as his fingers trailed lower and feathered across the pouting puff of filmy fabric between her legs.

'And you're already wet for me,' he whispered, his other hand moving around her back, fumbling to unhook the half-cup bra and toss it aside, allowing the splendour of her pink-tipped breasts to tumble free. His fingers flew to the buttons of his shirt and with a surge of dizzying excitement she saw that they were shaking, so she reached up to help him tear it open, gasping as the shirt joined her scattered clothes on the floor.

'What's the matter?' he said, sweeping his hands down her naked back to settle around her waist, drawing her towards the strong columns of his thighs.

'Nothing,' she said huskily, plunging her hands into the rich, dark thicket of hair that spread between the shiny bronze discs of his nipples and tugging at it to make him groan. 'I just thought that you were smooth-chested…'

'Shall I stop and shave?' he teased raggedly, but she detected the faint note of chagrin and hastened to reassure him. How could she have known his self-confidence was so fragile? she thought with a secret smile.

'Oh, no, I like you like this,' she said, letting him see how she frankly gloried in his rampant masculinity, kneading his chest hair like a purring kitten, bending to pull at it with her teeth, and nuzzling through the curling strands to find his flat nipples with her tongue, eager for a taste of him.

He reacted with savage eroticism, returning the heated favour, gathering her in with his strong arms and rubbing the fur on his chest against her bare breasts until the exciting friction made her beg for surcease, whereupon he arched her backwards and took them in his scalding mouth, sucking at the nipples until they were tight, hard, little berries, bursting with hot sensation.

'You taste of salt,' he growled, moving back up her throat to savour her mouth and ears and eyes, everywhere the sea spray had dissolved on her skin.

She licked at his jaw, her darting tongue causing the muscle to flicker and clench. 'Mmm, so do you,' she whispered approvingly.

He swung her up in his arms in spite of her squeak of feverish protest about her weight, and carried her with laughing ease into his bedroom, stripping back the bedclothes before laying her on her back on the cool white sheets. She stretched, bending her arms back over her head and restlessly shifting her legs as he stood and unbuckled his belt and shed both jeans and underwear in a single movement, his boldly jutting erection swaying as he knelt on the edge of the bed and threw his other knee to the mattress on the other side of her, straddling her with his powerful thighs. His hands caressingly encircled her waist and he tugged her down on the bed so that his mouth could reach her breasts, his thick shaft nudging into her softly rounded belly until he reached down and guided it to tease against the filmy-wet fabric between her legs.

'How much I'm going to enjoy entering my very private little rose garden,' he gloated silkily, rocking his hips. He smiled down into her hectically flushed face. 'You were in here, weren't you, Emily? In my bedroom…that's the only way you could have seen my *other* secret rose garden—there's no view or access to it except from this room. Were you lying here on my bed, having wicked thoughts about me, imagining me making love to you like this, touching you here….and here…and *especially* here…'

A burst of molten sparks showered through her at the delicate pressure against the heart of her femininity. She shuddered, her fingers curling into the rippling striations of hard muscle along his lean sides.

'I pretended your pillow was you…' she confessed foolishly in a fever of desiring, and his body shook with a sensuous chuckle.

'And did I feel like this…' he taunted, taking her hand and wrapping it around his hardness, coaxing her thumb to move, letting her feel the satiny heat and pulsing throb of the prominent head as he pushed himself against her eager fingers.

She moaned and he tugged the panties down her legs, helping her thresh to get rid of them, digging into the drawer beside his bed to curse his way impatiently into a condom, and then he was rolling over on his back, dragging her with him, setting her astride him, testing the hardness she had explored against her naked heat.

'Like this, I want to see you, I want to taste you and play with you while I'm inside you,' he said, cupping her breasts and fondling them, bending his knees to tilt the centre of her body over his erection, groaning as she began to slide down onto his rigid shaft. 'Yes, that's right, just like that…now love me…' he commanded hoarsely.

Love me. Her heart exploded with joy. If he wanted her to love him, perhaps he was ready to give the same gift in return. 'I do…I am…' she panted, crying out in frustration as her distended body briefly resisted his bold intrusion.

'Wait, Emily—am I hurting you?' He froze, his big frame rock-hard with leashed sexual tension, gritting his teeth in tortured ecstasy as her sheath fisted around him. 'You're so damned…exquisitely, tight…'

'And you're so exquisitely…*right*…' she sighed. Her body had already recognised the lover of her dreams and with a sinuous twist that made him sweat and groan she took him completely, bowing over him, her swollen, blue-veined breasts brushing tantalisingly against his mouth until he lifted his head and captured them with his lips, holding her fast so that he could drink lustily from her sweetness, his big hands cupping her hips, urging her to a faster rhythm until her head fell back and her spine began to stiffen. Immediately one of his hands slid between their bodies to the place where they were joined and found the tiny, engorged bud of carnal pleasure, his skilled play bringing a violent flowering of drenching delight.

But still that wasn't enough for him, and even as she was still racked with shivering convulsions he rolled her over, reversing their positions, rising above her on braced arms and accelerating the driving thrusts of his powerful hips until she twined her legs around his waist and screamed in another shattering climax, feeling the violent, pulsing spasm of his thickened shaft as he joined her in a prolonged outpouring of voluptuous gratification.

Afterwards they lay locked in each other's arms, too lazy to move, perspiration cooling on their bodies as they drifted in and out of a satiated doze.

Each time she roused, she saw his well-loved face on the next pillow, and a sweet contentment that had nothing to do with her physical euphoria pierced her heart. Of course, the physical part was nice too, she thought with a secret smile.

'What are you thinking?'

Her lashes fluttered up to find his head propped on his hand, his eyes on her curved mouth.

Caught out, she blushed, but never thought of not telling him the stark truth. 'That I've never been so uninhibited before.'

Her blush deepened as his silvered eyes darkened with arrogant satisfaction, his eyes smouldering as he looked at her rosy, well-suckled breasts, and the sheen of their exertions still burnishing her soft belly and thighs. 'You've never made love with *me* before,' he said lazily, his hand lying possessively on her hip. 'We've still got a lot to discover about each other, but at least we know we make a hell of a combination in bed.'

He didn't utter words of newly realised love, and so Emily didn't either, suddenly less certain than she had been a few minutes before. She had told him she loved him in the throes of their passion, if he wasn't going to reciprocate unprompted then she wasn't going to embarrass herself by begging. She would sound too needy. At least his words bespoke a future. She would just have to wait, and hope...

'What time do you want to fly back to Auckland?' she asked, wondering how long she could make their precious idyll last.

His hand swirled on her hip, a strange smile crossing his lips. 'Do you know what that sound is?'

She realised the once bright and airy room had got dim, even though sunset must still be some way away. She listened and heard the swirling patter of rain against the leaves outside a window, a distant crash of rolling thunder. The helicopter was obviously grounded for the duration.

'Heaven?' She smiled, a slow, sensual, inviting smile.

He laughed. 'A predicted twelve-hour weather front,' he confirmed, moving his hand somewhere far more intimate. 'So...heaven, it is, then...'

And later, after he had shown her that she had many other ways to be joyously uninhibited in his arms, he had relented on his total rejection of the earthly world, and, tucked together like spoons, they had talked about Peter's implacable conviction that she was Carol's daughter.

Emily pushed her phone call with her mother to the back of her mind, but admitted with a sigh: 'If it turns out I *am* adopted, I suppose it would explain a lot of things about my parents…'

'Emotionally detached from you?' he guessed, his chest sending vibrations all down her lax spine.

'No, more that they're just equally emotionally attached to everyone,' she said, trying to find the words to explain. 'When I was a child I always felt I was in a sibling rivalry with all poor unfortunates of the world. I felt I'd never get their full attention unless I was a traumatic victim of some sort. Once I was no longer a helpless baby, totally reliant on their care, they felt they'd done their job as parents and I was pretty much left to my own devices. It's scary to be that free when you're little—I much preferred my grandparents' rigid rules—' She faltered. 'Or the people whom I *think* are my grandparents.'

'They'll always be that, adoptive or otherwise. In fact, you're amazingly normal for someone with such a bizarre family pathology,' he said.

'Is that supposed to be reassuring?' She giggled, wriggling her bottom more securely into the spoon of his hips. '*Your* family isn't exactly turning out to be run-of-the-mill.'

'Yes, Dylan does tend to rather run me *through* the mill for his own entertainment,' he grumbled, gently nipping the tender rim of her ear. 'I suppose he thought it was a great joke, taunting me with the fact he was smuggling you into my house.'

'He never said. What was in the text?' she asked curiously.

'Well, it started off with "Once aboard the lugger the girl is mine."' he said, giving her another admonishing nip as her body jiggled with giggles. 'Young idiot. What did he expect me to do?'

'Probably precisely what you did do,' she guessed. 'He seemed awfully eager to hang around once we got here. He said it would be cool if I was his metaphorical sister,' she added.

Ethan choked. 'Good. Even metaphorically, Dylan wouldn't sink to incest.'

But when she tried to talk to him about Peter's will, as they ate barbecued steaks on the enclosed deck while the rain lashed around the shutters, he refused to get involved.

'But I think for both your sakes you should go for a DNA test as soon as possible. Then let the cards fall how they may.'

She fretted at his reticence, her brow wrinkling. He had said the money didn't bother him, but something did... She knew he was angry with Peter, but she wasn't sure whether it was because of the old affair and its consequences, or his recent actions—or a painful combination of both. She didn't want to get between Ethan and his uncle, but it seemed that she didn't have any choice. And now, by becoming Ethan's lover, she had complicated the tangle of conflicting loyalties even further.

She was wondering whether she should risk her new status by forcing the subject out into the open when he casually dropped his bombshell.

'By the way, in all the toil and trouble I never got to tell you. I talked to Tremaine—*and* his boss—and *his* boss. If you give me your bank account number, the full indemnity value of your house as listed in your policy will be paid into your bank account by the end of the week. And there's a construction crew ready to move in tomorrow and start rebuilding from the original plans. You should have your home back to a better-than-pristine state in six weeks, max.'

She stared at him with an open mouth. Just when she was having doubts about him he conjured a miracle that showed how much he really *did* care, working quietly behind the scenes to move mountains in her honour.

He leaned over and tapped her jaw shut. 'Yes, I know. I'm a genius. That's why you—you think I'm wonderful.'

That's why you love me.

He wouldn't even use the casual cliché, because he knew it was neither casual, nor a cliché as far as Emily was concerned.

If he said it, and she agreed, then the next words would have to come from him, and Ethan didn't use the word love lightly.

He couldn't be bullied, seduced, or conned into saying it.

But he might—just might—be *loved* into it...

CHAPTER TEN

EMILY was applying gold leaf to the gold-trimmed lattice work of a hand-painted dinner plate when the door to the studio rattled open and Mrs Cooper made an unprecedented entrance.

Alarmed by her huffing and puffing as she tried to speak, Emily pulled off her magnifying spectacles and eased back on her stool so as not to disturb the delicate sheets of gold leaf that she had laid out for matching to the two other plates that were next in line for re-gilding.

'What's the matter? Is it Peter?' she asked worriedly and Mrs Cooper shook her head.

'There's a phone call for you,' she panted. 'Mr Nash said to hurry. He said it was from Africa. He said it was your mother on the line.'

'Oh!' Abandoning her tools, Emily took to her heels, hoping that the connection wouldn't be lost before she got there, leaving Mrs Cooper to close the door to the studio and follow at the more leisurely pace.

It had been over a week since she had spoken to her mother, and, given the nature of her parents' posting, she had known it was futile to fret and fury at the lack of communication. Since Peter had been pressing her, and it made her uncomfortable that he was trying to act as if the fact she was his granddaughter was a foregone conclusion, she had told him that she had asked about the circumstances of her birth and now it was just a matter of patiently awaiting the reply. As she had pointed out, time had a different meaning in her parents' world—urgency was based on physical need, with the simple need-to-know very far down on their list of priorities. She certainly wasn't going to take a DNA test until it became the logical next step. Secretly, Emily hadn't minded being suspended in the strange kind of identity-limbo, for it meant she could just push all her doubts away and devote her attention to the other, even more incredible development in her life.

For her burgeoning relationship with Ethan, the week had been one of guilty pleasure and unalloyed happiness. After their stay on Waiheke Island they had spent most of their evenings together, and, even though she felt a little uncomfortable about deceiving Peter, each night after he retired she would sneak along to make love in Ethan's big bed, and sleep cuddled in his arms until dawn streaked the room with golden light. Once, they'd both overslept, and Mrs Cooper had caught her creeping out his door to the verandah in order to nip back along to her room without being seen, but since Ethan could do no wrong as far as the housekeeper was concerned she had primly turned a blind eye to what she termed their 'shenanigans'.

Dylan, meanwhile, had returned to his apartment when his actor-tenant and family had flown back to Hollywood, leaving him much the richer for their visit. Without his boisterous and distracting presence, Emily and Ethan had been free to concentrate on each other...to tease and talk and engage in the age-old game of sensual love-play, while instinctively getting to know one another on a deeper level.

Ethan had even opened up about the traumatic set of circumstances that had led to his fear of flying, touching on the subject of his broken engagement with a hint of residual bitterness that told Emily that his youthful heart had been very much involved, and that he still bore the scars. It was evident that both experiences were strongly associated with each other in his mind, doubling their impact on his psyche. No wonder he had developed such an extreme emotional wariness. To Ethan, love, rejection, grief and loss were all inextricably mixed up together.

Now he had flown out to a new site for a few days, and Emily was coping with her own temporary sense of loss, and the troubling realisation that, in concealing her love as if it were an embarrassment rather than openly celebrating it with him, she might be actively supporting him in his emotional hibernation. He had conquered his fear of flying, but no one had yet given him sufficient incentive to conquer his fear of love.

'In here!' Peter called from his office, and limped around the desk, eagerly holding up the cordless receiver for her as she hurried into the room.

'It's my mother? Are you sure? The static made it hard to tell last time I spoke to her,' she said as she grabbed it and held it to her chest, knowing she was only putting off the moment of truth.

'It's as clear as a bell,' he said. He hesitated, his face both excited and strained. 'I should go and let you talk to her,' he said, his bony hands clenching at his sides.

'No—yes. No!' She caught his arm, and sank into the leather chair in front of the desk on weak knees, her heart beating like a drum. It wasn't fair to draw out his agonised wait, and she suddenly didn't want to be alone. She wished Ethan were here, with his rock-solid presence and cool detachment.

'Please. You may as well stay and listen.' She took a deep breath and raised the receiver. 'Hello, Mum?'

Peter leant on the edge of his desk as he listened to the frustratingly one-sided conversation and when she finally handed him the disconnected receiver, her other hand spread over her face, there were weak tears in his eyes and a tight dread in his chest.

'So you *were* adopted,' he acknowledged heavily, letting the receiver clatter to the desk.

She nodded behind her hands, tears leaking out through her splayed fingers as she leaned her elbows on her knees.

'But you're not my granddaughter after all, are you, Emily?' he continued wretchedly, looking down at her brown curls.

She shook her head, sucking in a shuddering breath as she dropped her hands and looked up, hurting for him as much as for herself. 'They'd never heard of anyone of your daughter's description, not in their particular group, anyway,' she recounted raggedly. 'But it was a hugely chaotic time and lots of comings and goings were never recorded, and the usual corruption and bribery was always available to get things done.'

She straightened her spine. 'My real mother was one of my parents' best friends—another aid worker. She was—she'd been brutally raped and hadn't told anyone, then was horrified to find she was pregnant.' She choked to a halt and forced herself to go on: 'She couldn't have an abortion because of her faith, but she couldn't bear to keep the baby—to keep me—and nor could she just abandon me in a foreign orphanage, so Mum and Dad did their good deed. They simply claimed me as their own, and then bribed some people to forge papers so they could get me onto their own passports.'

She smiled crookedly, wiping her drenched eyes. 'So that's why they never told me—they were afraid if anyone found out it could jeopardise their work, they could even go to prison for immigration offences, and my right to citizenship might be revoked. They thought it was safer if everyone believed I was their biological daughter—even their own parents. They were travelling around so much the lies were all very plausible. And they didn't see the point in telling me that my real mother never wanted to meet me, and my father was just some anonymous rapist.'

Her voice broke up as she stood and looked into his drawn face. His skin was grey and he looked to have aged ten years. 'I'm sorry, Peter. I know how very much you wanted this—but I'm definitely not Carol's daughter. I'm not the person you've been looking for…'

'But you're the one that I found,' he said remorsefully, suddenly pulling her into a fierce bear-hug. 'Our friendship's still real, even if the other's not. *I'm* the one who's sorry, Emily. Sorry for being such a wrong-headed, stubborn old fool and refusing to listen to reason. I can see now how I let my hopes grow into obsession that warped my views. Everything I was told

I just twisted to fit my preconceptions. If I hadn't seized the wrong end of the stick years ago you wouldn't be going through all this mental anguish now. You would still have been in blissful ignorance about your parentage. I had no right to try and play God with your life.'

It was her turn to pat his back and try to find words that might console him. 'You know what they say about the truth setting you free,' she said lamely, although she thought it might take a while for her to believe it.

They shed a few more tears together and then, sensing he needed time alone to grieve for the death of his hopes, Emily insisted on going back to work, but once in the studio she tidied everything away and sat staring into space. Everything was the same, yet everything had changed. Peter was adamant that this wouldn't affect their friendship, but inevitably it must. He would never give up. He had had a shock and a setback, but eventually he would want to start searching for his lost granddaughter again. And next time he might well be successful. Stranger things had happened. Like Emily Quest turning out to be Emily No-name!

For Peter's sake she pretended to eat her dinner with her normal enthusiasm, but she noticed that both of them were merely shifting the food around their plates to disguise their lack of appetite, and the conversation faltered awkwardly as they tried to avoid the more painful aspects of the topic that was so much on their minds. She knew he was unhappy with the decision that she had just announced, but equally she knew that it was the right thing for her to do.

The next afternoon she was quietly transferring her books from the shelf in her bedroom into a slightly water-stained gear bag when a sudden electric change in the atmosphere made her skin prickle.

Ethan was standing silently in the open French doors to the verandah, watching her with sombre eyes.

'Ethan—' she sighed. She should have known.

'Uncle Peter called to tell me what happened,' he said, confirming her suspicion. Despite all their sneaking around and his claims to be a foolish old man, Peter wasn't stupid.

'He dragged you away from your work—'

'I was coming back this evening, anyway,' he said, stepping across the threshold and looking at the books. 'He said you were going back to squat in your half-built house. Were you planning to be gone before I got back?'

He was implying she was running away. 'No, Ethan, it's not like that—'

'What is it like, then?'

She pushed a hand through her hair, her smile wobbling as she trotted out a masterly understatement: 'Rather awful, actually.'

He held out his arms and she flew home.

'Damn it!' he ground out against her curls as she buried her face against his chest. 'This is exactly what I was afraid would happen.'

'What—that I would turn out to be a complete impostor?' she asked in a muffled voice.

'No—that this would end up in a world of hurt for someone.'

She lifted her head. 'I think Peter needs your sympathy as much as I do. He feels terrible.'

That's why he doesn't want you to leave.'

She unwrapped herself reluctantly from his arms and stood back. 'I can't stay, you must see that. Peter really only asked me to move in because he thought I was his own flesh and blood. My staying here is just going to make the truth more difficult and painful to accept—for both of us. I don't want to strain our friendship like that. It's not as if I'm completely disappearing on him—I'll still be coming here to work every day until my studio is rebuilt. But now I have the money to support myself and have replaced my car, there's no good reason for me not to go back home. The cleaners have been through and my bedroom's perfectly habitable, the bathroom's functional and the electrical wiring and plumbing has all been done so I have power and running water.'

'Habitable but hardly comfortable. Haven't the carpet and curtains been taken to the dump and all the wallpaper stripped?'

'I don't mind roughing it until the builders finish and I can redecorate,' she said, picking up another book, trying to sound strong and independent.

Ethan was staring at her broodingly. 'If your scruples won't let you stay here, why don't you come with me to Waiheke?' he said abruptly. 'You could commute by ferry every day. It wouldn't take you much longer than it does from your house.'

The book fell with a thump from her nerveless fingers.

'Are you asking me to move in with you?' she asked, in a hushed voice of breathless eagerness. 'To live with you?'

There was a profound silence in which she thought she could hear the sound of her blood pumping sluggishly through her oxygen-starved heart.

Oh, God, she might just as well have asked him for a ring!

'Well, to stay until your house is finished, anyway,' Ethan temporised, the sudden wariness in his eyes offset by a sexy smile, reminding her of what she'd be missing if she refused.

Her chugging blood thinned rapidly, flowing out to her skin from her stricken heart, turning hope to an embarrassed flush. She should have known it was too good to be true. Of course he hadn't been suggesting anything remotely permanent. He had simply made an impulsive offer designed to promote the convenience of their affair, safe in the knowledge he would be waving her goodbye in a few weeks, when the sex got stale.

Now he had even more reasons to be wary. Perhaps it had belatedly occurred to him that he would be giving house room to the daughter of a rapist? After all, who knew what bad blood might flow through her mongrel veins!

Emily knew she was being grossly unfair, but was too hurt to care.

'Then, thanks, but I think I'd rather settle in at my own place,' she said lightly, over the sound of her cracking heart. She picked up the fallen book. 'I'd always planned on moving back there as soon as I could. I never wanted to impose on anyone—'

'You wouldn't be imposing.' Ethan's smile faded to a frown. 'Don't you want to come? I thought you said you liked the place.'

'I did.' Liked the place, loved the owner. Hated that he her made her feel unworthy of any future with him.

She put the book into the bag and turned. Ethan moved into her path, his fingers hooking under the straps of her vest-top and stretching them lightly, pulling the ribbed fabric tight across her breasts. 'I could make you say yes,' he murmured seductively. He bent his head and nuzzled the side of her throat. 'I think we both know I could very easily make you change your mind.'

She fought down her weak desire to do just that. He was trying to make this all about sex, and she couldn't let him get away with it. 'Yes, you could,' she admitted huskily. 'But would you want to, knowing what it would mean to me?'

He raised his head, arrested by the painful throb in her voice. She met his gaze proudly, her heart in her eyes. 'So unless you're ready to take responsibility for that, maybe you should agree that separate residences are safer for both of us…'

For a moment she almost believed—hoped—that he was going to argue, but then he inclined his head, and let the precious moment slide.

'Of course, it's entirely your choice. Now you have your insurance money you don't have to accept unwelcome favours from men.'

It was a cheap shot, and from the sudden high colour on his cheekbones, he knew it, and her own wounded heart ached for him as he spun on his heel and left. But she was fairly sure that he would swiftly recover his arrogant confidence once he analysed the scene and realised that it was as a landlord rather than a lover that he had been rejected. The passion that flared so hot between them was still his for the taking, and the fact that she had obliquely warned him that she was falling in love with him might merely add an extra element of challenge to the affair. At least he would know that she wasn't trying to line him up for an emotional ambush, or trade on his generosity.

After a few days of the new regime she wouldn't admit, even to herself, that her home no longer seemed to fit her any more. It was as if the fire had consumed its spirit and the seismic shift that had taken place in her own identity and emotions contributed to her feelings of restless displacement. Work no longer filled the empty gaps in her life. The question nagged at her—would James Quest have left her everything if he'd known she wasn't his biological granddaughter? She'd like to think that the answer was yes, that her life with him had more than earned his love and respect for her as a person of value in her own right, but she was no longer sure of anything. It would probably take years to resolve all the issues and conflicted feelings arising from the discovery of her birth. Each time she spoke to or saw her parents, her *adoptive* parents, she would undoubtedly have a long list of questions to ask them.

Apart from the inconveniences of open walls and the thick coating of builder's dust that renewed itself every day and drifted into every nook and cranny, Emily found the stripped-down house echoing and hollow, and more than a little spooky when the sun went down.

On her first night she had been shedding a few tears into her pillow when her mobile phone screen had flashed a welcome light in the dark. She had snatched it up to hear a gravelly purr.

'In bed yet?'

She pinched the top of her nose so he wouldn't hear the tears. 'Who is this?'

'Very funny. Have you got so many lovers you can't distinguish one from the other?'

Lovers. Tears, this time of relief, threatened anew.

'I wish!'

'No, you don't.' Oh, he had got all his arrogance back, and then some! 'How are you getting on? Finding it a bit sad and lonely?'

It was so accurate she was incensed. 'I was asleep,' she lied.

'So you *are* in bed. What are you wearing?'

Her nipples instantly peaked against her silk camisole. He knew she liked to wear pretty things to bed.

'Striped flannel pyjamas.'

'Liar,' he chuckled. 'Aren't you going to ask me what I'm wearing?'

He slept naked.

'No. Where are you?' she asked helplessly, picturing his nude body sprawled across the big bed overlooking the secret rose garden. Perhaps he was even stroking himself as he talked to her, she thought with a shocking spurt of heat between her legs.

'I had to fly back down to the site. I'm bunking in with one of my drainage engineers,' he said, shattering her wicked fantasy. 'Have you changed your mind, yet?'

So that was the way he was going to play it.

'No, have you?'

Silence.

'Goodnight, Emily.'

'Goodnight, Ethan.'

He had called her the next two nights as well, and each time he had ended their long, meandering conversations in the same way. She wondered whether the fact he was choosing to taunt her with a reminder that she loved him was significant. It was another two days before he was due to return, and she found herself looking forward to two more intimate, late-night conversations almost as much as his teasing threats of a love-making marathon. Never having considered herself very highly sexed, she was disconcerted at how much she had missed the purely physical side of their relationship and how much time she wasted dreaming up torrid sex scenes in which to satisfy her craving for his erotic skills.

The next afternoon she had returned home early to supervise the delivery of her new kitchen appliances and was flattening cartons in the front yard for the recycling collection when she was amused to see Peter drive up in his yellow 'runabout'.

'I hope you aren't going to put Jeff out of his job,' she greeted him as he picked his way around the piles of builder's debris that she had been assured would be cleared away at the end of the job.

'He's at the chiropractor's. Disc bulge,' he announced. 'It's not a patch on the Rolls, of course, but it's quite a zippy little thing, isn't it?' he said, patting the roof with smug satisfaction. 'I just thought I'd come around and see how things are going.'

After she had shown him around and given him a cup of tea, she walked him back to his car.

'I haven't taken you out of my will, you know,' he said abruptly and she looked at him in consternation. 'And I'm not going to!'

'Peter—!'

'I know, I know. You're not my granddaughter. I know that. But I've thought about it, and I want you to know you're as good as a granddaughter to me, even though we're not related. As I told you I've got pots of money, and I've already had Robinson set up a separate trust-fund for Carol's daughter whoever she might turn out to be. And if you're worried about the boys, don't be—I've told them all about it and they're happy as Larry, both of them. Said you deserve it after all the strife I caused. But I'm not giving it to you as reparation or a bribe,' he insisted as she opened her mouth, 'I'm giving it to you because it makes me happy to think of you having it after I'm gone. You want me to die happy, don't you?'

'I don't want you to die at all!' she said, thinking that he seemed to have recovered a lot of his former spryness.

'Then don't put more stress on my ticker by arguing with me,' he told her, deftly getting the last word. He looked back at the house, where the sounds of an electric drill and a nail-gun competed for supremacy.

'No one better than Ethan's crew at pulling a top-rate job together in record time,' he said, nodding with pride. 'That tow-headed one on the roof—Shorty—he's been with Ethan since the day he started his first house.'

'*Ethan's* boys?' Emily's eyes jerked from Peter to the man hammering down sheets of corrugated steel roofing. 'But they're from an outfit called Jacad Construction. I presumed they'd got the job by offering the insurance company the cheapest quote—'

'Jacad's one of Ethan's subsidiary companies. I think you'll find he was the one who set everything up and rammed it all through so quickly. They're top-notch specialists and usually charge like wounded bulls, so no way are they going to be the cheapest quote to some cheap-jack insurance company, not unless someone is subsidising their bills—'

Emily was shell-shocked into stammering confusion. 'Are—are you saying that *Ethan*…?'

'Did you ever talk to that insurance man again yourself?'

'Well, no…Ethan said—Ethan said he'd handle it,' she finished slowly, her eyes widening.

Peter nodded, his shock of white hair almost luminous in the sun. 'And so he did. I also happen to know that he's still battling the insurance people over the size of the indemnity. So that direct-deposit you were so happy about—I think you'll maybe find it didn't originate from any insurance fund.'

Ethan?

'But—I don't understand—why would he *do* that?' she wailed. Just when she thought she had him all figured out, the man turned back into a riddle!

'That's a fascinating question. Why don't you ask him next time you see him?' said Peter, getting back behind the wheel of his car, having done what he came to do, hoping that his irrepressible desire to meddle wasn't going to backfire on him again. Emily wasn't his granddaughter, but he had high hopes she might still turn out to be a member of the family.

Emily waited impatiently until Shorty came off the roof and then subjected him to a pointed conversation, which confirmed that Ethan, and not her insurance company, had fast-tracked the reconstruction job, and the bills were all being sent to an off-shore investment company, which, surprise surprise, was the same one that funded Ethan's speculative building projects.

That night she forced herself to switch her mobile phone off and lay awake twisting and turning, fighting the urgent desire to check for messages every few minutes. In her mind she was going over and over the events of the past few weeks, inspecting each and every incident for new significance, wondering if it had been her own doubts and uncertainties she had been projecting onto Ethan, rather than accepting him as the man he truly was; expecting perfection when she was far from perfect herself. Her craving for stability in an inherently unstable world was foolish if it meant that she was rejecting the one thing that she wanted above all else. In trying to fit the small, jigsaw pieces of her broken life back together she had been ignoring the big picture. What she had been doing was conservation, not restoration. Conservation was about preserving an object in its existing damaged condition, restoration was about infusing that object with new and vigorous life for the future.

Once she had made up her mind she was actually able to sleep for a few hours, and early the next morning she phoned Dylan to ask if he still had the keys to Ethan's house.

Only with difficulty did she stop him from inserting himself into the plan and embellishing it with outrageous ideas. Even then, when she met him down by the waterfront to pick up the keys, she was tempted to let down the tyres of his Porsche to stop him from following her onto the car ferry. In typical fashion he had dressed up in a double-breasted trench coat and hat, and sidled up to talk out of the side of his mouth as he passed her a slip of paper with the directions to Ethan's house and security code.

'Make sure you eat it when you've memorised it,' he said. 'You'll notice I spread marmalade on the back to make it go down more easily.'

Sure enough there was a sticky blob that tasted of grapefruit when she licked it off her finger. He had obviously scribbled down the address at the breakfast table.

'No invisible ink?'

He grinned. 'I ran out of lemons.'

'I hope you're not going in to work like that,' she said disparagingly, slipping the note into the pocket of the swirling green sundress that she thought would nicely blend in with the summer crowd on the island.

'I thought I looked like one of those sexy spies you see in old-fashioned movies.'

'Inspector Clouseau, more like,' she muttered, half expecting him to break out in an excruciating French accent like the fictional detective.

Fortunately his directions proved to be straightforward rather than the convoluted tour of the island she had half expected from his costume, and the security code exactly correct.

The house was enfolded in a beautiful hush as she stepped inside, almost as if it had been waiting for her to arrive, and she left her sandals by the door as she prowled on her mission, eventually settling on the white stone mantelpiece under a painting of a stark blue sea.

'What are you doing?'

Emily jumped and uttered a shriek of alarm, only just managing to catch the small lidded jar as it slipped from her fingers and almost crashed onto the hardwood floor.

'Oh, God, you're not supposed to be here—you scared me to death!' she told Ethan, feverishly inspecting the jar and lid for chips. 'I can't believe I almost let it fall!'

Ethan's eyebrows rose at her accusing tone. 'What is it?'

'A melon jar,' she said, shaken by the near miss, setting it carefully on the mantelpiece and positioning it to the best advantage.

'It's pretty small to hold a melon.'

She bristled at his mockery. 'It's called that because of the melon-vine pattern. It happens to be very valuable.'

'Really? That little thing? How much is it worth?'

She told him, the adrenalin of fear still racing around her body, making her feel punchy and light-headed.

He blinked and took another, much more respectful look at the jar. *'That much?'*

She tried to calm her galloping heart, feeling a kick of satisfaction at his incredulous shock.

'Yes. It's a very rare piece—fifteenth-century Chinese, with a fascinating imperial history. It was owned by a Dowager Empress who awarded it to a very influential British dignitary who was serving in China at the beginning of the twentieth century. My grandfather bought it over thirty years ago at a private auction. It was his most precious possession,' she said proudly.

An arrested expression crossed his face. 'Wait a minute! You mean to tell me you had this thing all along? I thought you were going to be broke until the insurance money came through?'

Emily looked puzzled, then appalled when she realised what he was suggesting. 'But I couldn't have *sold* it!' she cried in horror at the thought. 'It was Grandpa's pride and joy. He called it his "one true thing". It's literally priceless. I could *never* sell it. It's not a *commodity*, it's my history, my *heritage*…'

There was a stunned silence after her dramatic pronouncement, and Ethan's brief flare of outrage melted into a silky-smooth curiosity.

'So what's it doing here on my mantelpiece?'

Now that she had got over her initial fright, Emily suddenly realised that her careful plans had been thrown into total disarray. Her eyes widened as she also took in the full impact of Ethan's bare chest and unsnapped, low-slung jeans.

'I—I—what are you doing home, anyway?'

'I discovered I had some urgent personal business in town,' he said softly. 'So—up to some of your old tricks again, are you, Emily? Sneaking into people's houses and shifting around their possessions? Although I see you've skipped the fishnet stockings this time around…'

She flushed, becoming more unnerved by the minute. She ran her hand through her hair and his eyes registered the lift of her breasts against the thin bodice of her sundress.

'N-no—I didn't—I wanted to give you the melon jar,' she murmured. 'So I persuaded Dylan to lend me your key. I was going to leave it here as a surprise. I knew you'd know who it was from. Look at it, it's absolutely perfect for this room—simple and elegant—and the blue and white pattern stands out against your white wall and picks up the colours of the painting above it. And the vine pattern is a floral one,' she said, pointing out the delicate tracery, 'very appropriate for a man who grows roses—'

'You want to give me your heritage?' he said quietly, interrupting her nervous commentary.

'You seem to be giving me some of yours.' They might as well get it all out in the open. 'Your construction crew—the insurance money—I know all about it,' she said wildly.

'Do you? I doubt it.' He put his hand on the mantel. 'So this is just a kind of repayment, then—a quid pro quo because you can't bear the idea of being in debt to me?'

If she agreed, that would be defeating the whole purpose of her generosity. *'No!* I told you, its intrinsic value has nothing to do with money. It's a gift,' she declared, 'from me to you.'

He smiled, the tight angles of his face softening, his ice-blue eyes acquiring a warm patina. 'Another one? Don't you remember? You've already given me a rare gift.'

Her brow wrinkled.

'Something even more precious than this,' he said, stroking the curve of the jar with a delicacy that appreciated its subtle beauty.

She shook her head, mystified. She *had* nothing more precious, she thought as he picked up her hands, drawing her away towards the middle of the room, towards the long, white couch scattered with jewel-bright cushions.

He halted in a pool of sunlight that mantled his powerful shoulders in a cloak of gold and lifted her hands to the warm mat of hair on his chest, letting her feel the unsteady thud of his heart. 'Something you could never sell, you could only give away. Your own "one, true thing", Emily…'

Realisation dawned. Her breath caught in her throat at the tender understanding in his eyes, the passionate conviction in his voice. As usual, he was already one step ahead of her. 'Oh! Oh, *that…*'

'And instead of honouring the gift you gave me, I used you.'

She felt a twist of pain. Had she misread him? 'No—'

'Yes, because I enjoyed having you love me, even while I pretended I didn't want to know.

'You made me feel too much, Emily, and that frightened me—it took me back to a time in my life when I felt utterly helpless to control the emotional chaos inside me—so I kept throwing up roadblocks, trying to find reasons to dislike you, to hold back—to not allow myself to find you sexy, funny, attractive, kind, sweet…not to see you as you really were, not to want you. And when that didn't work, it was so much easier to reduce it to sex, to call it passion or desire, because then I could walk away from it if I chose, the way I always had before.

'But I can't walk away from you, Emily,' he said quietly, placing his hand along her cheek, his thumb brushing across her lips. 'I tried it and it didn't work,' he admitted ruefully. 'You're too much a part of *me*—a part I don't want to deny any more. You didn't answer your phone last night and I nearly went crazy worrying about what might have happened. I almost rang Dylan to ask him to check on you for me, but I knew he'd laugh me off the phone.'

'Peter told me about the insurance money. I was brooding,' she confessed. 'And plotting my revenge,' she added, looking at him under her lashes.

'I gave you the money in part because I wanted you to be totally free to make your own choices, not feel trapped by Peter's expectations—or mine,' he said. 'But I admit that there was also an element of manipulation. I enjoyed feeling in control—knowing I was helping you without having to explain why I felt the need to do so. What I really wanted was for you to be free to choose to be with me.'

'I already had chosen you,' she reminded him huskily. She moved her hands over his chest, feeling his heartbeat accelerate. 'I loved you so much you made me tongue-tied. Last night I decided that it was time I laid my heart on the line. I let you stop me saying the words because I was afraid of losing you. That jar was a message that you mean more to me than all the pots in China.'

His mouth curved at her solemn sincerity. 'And you mean more to me than all the roses in my garden,' he teased.

'In spite of my sordid beginnings?' she asked hesitantly.

'I'm just grateful to whoever gave you life, because that life has finally put you here, where you belong,' he said simply.

She slid her arms slid around his waist, revelling in the feel of his hot satin skin, her eyes iridescent with joy. 'Do you mean that?'

He tipped up her head, his hard mouth moving passionately over her pliant lips, half smothering the long-awaited words.

'I mean that I love you, Ms West,' she thought she heard him say.

Her loving laughter echoed in the warm cavern of his mouth. 'That's *Quest,* not *West.*'

He fell down with her onto the white couch and lay her against his heart. 'What say we clear up that potential confusion for once and for all?'

'And how do you propose to do that?' she invited huskily, linking her arms around his neck.

His eyes gleamed with wicked humour. 'Why, by proposing, of course…that we get rid of that pesky and divisive Q!'

Don't miss the brilliant
new novel from

Natalie Rivers

**featuring a dark, dangerous
and decadent Italian!**

THE SALVATORE
MARRIAGE DEAL

Available June 2008
Book #2735

*Look out for more books
from Natalie Rivers coming soon,
only in Harlequin Presents!*

HARLEQUIN® *Presents*®

What do you look for in a guy?
Charisma. Sex appeal. Confidence.
A body to die for. Well, look no further
this series has men with all this and more!
And now that they've met the women in these novels,
there is one thing on everyone's mind….

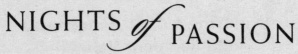
NIGHTS *of* PASSION

One night is never enough!

**The guys know what they want
and how they're going to get it!**

Don't miss:
HIS MISTRESS
BY ARRANGEMENT
by
Natalie Anderson
Available June 2008.

*Look out for more Nights of Passion,
coming soon in Harlequin Presents!*

Harlequin Presents brings you
a brand-new duet by star author

Sharon Kendrick

THE GREEK BILLIONAIRES' BRIDES

Power, pride and passion—discover how only
the love and passion of two women can reunite
these wealthy, successful brothers,
divided by a bitter rivalry.

Available June 2008:

THE GREEK TYCOON'S BABY BARGAIN

Available July 2008:

THE GREEK TYCOON'S CONVENIENT WIFE

REQUEST YOUR FREE BOOKS!

2 FREE NOVELS
PLUS 2
FREE GIFTS!

YES! Please send me 2 FREE Harlequin Presents® novels and my 2 FREE gifts (gifts are worth about $10). After receiving them, if I don't wish to receive any more books, I can return the shipping statement marked "cancel". If I don't cancel, I will receive 6 brand-new novels every month and be billed just $4.05 per book in the U.S. or $4.74 per book in Canada, plus 25¢ shipping and handling per book and applicable taxes, if any*. That's a savings of close to 15% off the cover price! I understand that accepting the 2 free books and gifts places me under no obligation to buy anything. I can always return a shipment and cancel at any time. Even if I never buy another book, the two free books and gifts are mine to keep forever.   106 HDN ERRW   306 HDN ERRL

Name _____ (PLEASE PRINT) _____

Address _____ Apt. # _____

City _____ State/Prov. _____ Zip/Postal Code _____

Signature (if under 18, a parent or guardian must sign) _____

Mail to the Harlequin Reader Service:
IN U.S.A.: P.O. Box 1867, Buffalo, NY 14240-1867
IN CANADA: P.O. Box 609, Fort Erie, Ontario L2A 5X3

Not valid to current subscribers of Harlequin Presents books.

Want to try two free books from another line?
Call 1-800-873-8635 or visit www.morefreebooks.com.

* Terms and prices subject to change without notice. N.Y. residents add applicable sales tax. Canadian residents will be charged applicable provincial taxes and GST. This offer is limited to one order per household. All orders subject to approval. Credit or debit balances in a customer's account(s) may be offset by any other outstanding balance owed by or to the customer. Please allow 4 to 6 weeks for delivery. Offer available while quantities last.

HP08

I ♥ HARLEQUIN® *Presents*

BROUGHT TO YOU BY FANS OF HARLEQUIN PRESENTS.

We are its editors and authors and biggest fans—and we'd love to hear from YOU!

Subscribe today to our online blog at
www.iheartpresents.com